RESOUNDING APPLAUSE

THE ANTIQUA PLAYERS
in Library of Crime Classics® editions:

THE PHILOMEL FOUNDATION

ELIZA'S GALIARDO

ELIZA'S GALIARDO

JAMES GOLLIN

INTERNATIONAL POLYGONICS, LTD.
New York

ELIZA'S GALIARDO

Library of Congress Card Catalog No. 86-81919
ISBN 0-930330-54-4

Printed and manufactured in the United States of America by Guinn Printing.
First IPL printing September 1986.
10 9 8 7 6 5 4 3 2 1

To the memory of
ROSE SCHWEIZER

I have endeavored in those my late Compositions to bring in a kind of Musick by which men might as it were Talk in Harmony . . .
    Giulio Caccini, Le Nuove Musiche
        (1601)

CHAPTER ONE

There are August mornings in New York City when the early sun sits up over the smog and haze like a half-chewed orange peel, about as lightgiving as the new high-intensity anticrime street-lights on my corner, the ones the lady in the Mayor's office is always forgetting to switch off at daybreak. String together ten or eleven of these mornings in a soggy row, and you know it's time to leave town. Sensible people toss their swimsuits, towels, and T-shirts into canvas carryalls and board the nearest air-conditioned conveyance to Elsewhere. Sensible people travel light and take things easy. We, however, are otherwise disposed. On this par-ticular August morning, three of us were delicately wrestling Ralph Mitchell's harpsichord into the service elevator of my build-ing. This wasn't Ralph's *biggest* harpsichord, you understand. The biggest is fifteen feet long, has a vulgar eighteenth-century paint-ing on the inside of the lid, and never goes anywhere. But this one is big enough and fragile enough to give us serious problems, the first one being that it's physically impossible to insert a concert harpsichord and three sweating musicians into a New York apart-ment-house back elevator.

"A little to the left. Good. Now tilt it." Ralph, in flip-flops and cutdown jeans, was superintending the operation, which had started at seven o'clock and was now into its second half-hour.

Meanwhile, Ramón the building super, who should have been helping us out, was pacing nervously back and forth in the service hall. I knew why. Ramón was fearful lest Ralph's harpsichord, heavily padded as it was, should somehow damage the sheet-steel walls or roof of the elevator. He was also nervous about leaving unwatched the thriving business in used tires and auto parts he and his cousin Incarnación were running out of several of the tenant storage bins in the basement.

By standing the harpsichord on its keyboard end and swearing at it, we finally squeezed it into the elevator car. Ralph and I rode down with it. You might think this was unnecessary, but with Ramón at the controls anything can happen. As the elevator careened down the shaftway from the ninth floor, I could see Ralph's lips moving in silent prayer. He was praying for a soft landing. Trying to fix a smashed harpsichord is like trying to reassemble Humpty-Dumpty himself, but a lot more expensive.

As soon as the car settled unsteadily on its shock absorbers, Ramón clattered open the gate and plunged off into the dimness. He was probably late for the morning trading session in hubcaps. A moment later, Terry and David rejoined us, and we started to work the harpsichord out of the elevator and up the treacherous basement steps to the street. We made it, panting, just as the horrible electric carillon at Saint Cecelia's began moaning out the eight-o'clock hymn. There was Jackie at the wheel of the big rented station wagon, which she'd somehow been able to park right in front of the service entrance. She scooted out and got the rear hatch open for us. The harpsichord slid into the interior as smoothly as a coffin glides into a hearse.

"Thank you very much," I said.

"Not at all," Jackie said, curtsying as they'd taught her when she was a little girl in Indiana. She was a big girl now, and in the shorts she was wearing to beat the heat her curtsy had an effect on me quite different from the one her teachers had had in mind. For a moment, all five of us stood on the sweltering pavement, happy to be done with a nasty little job. Then, Jackie began to laugh. "The Antiqua Players," she said. "Movers. Registered with the Interstate Commerce Commission. Alan French, foreman."

2

"There you go," said David.

I'm Alan French. David is David Brodkey, Terry is Terry Monza, Jackie is Jackie Craine, and Ralph Mitchell you've already met.

In case you haven't guessed, what we really are is performers of old music—medieval, Renaissance, Baroque—on old instruments with strange names. On viols and lute and harpsichord. On recorders and wooden flutes. On cornets and sackbuts and shawms and dolcians. In part because we're trained professionals and in part because we take this music seriously, we're very good at what we do. We've been playing as an ensemble for about five years. We've recorded, unfortunately on labels so obscure that even discomanes look blank at the names. We've toured in Europe, but that's another story.

Lately, business has been picking up. We're getting slightly more than our share of the pickings for early music groups. The reviewers are being kind. But don't be fooled. We still have to turn to other things to make a living.

Jackie teaches music at a girls' school on Long Island. She could easily make more money doing other things. Like modeling, for example. She's tall enough—about five-seven—and she certainly has the looks. Dark hair, creamy skin, blue, blue eyes, and a shape that attracts lively attention. But Jackie also has a brain in her head. Walking up and down a runway or in front of somebody's Hasselblad is not her idea of intellectual exercise. Besides, Jackie likes kids and gets a kick out of introducing them to real music. This is more than all right with me. Professionally and personally, I'm highly possessive about Jackie Craine.

I teach, too. And like hundreds of other New York musicians, I scramble after work in musical-comedy pit orchestras, pick-up studio recording bands and chamber groups. (Besides the early instruments, I play both violin and flute, which helps keep the bread and wine on the table.)

Ralph's industrialist father set up a trust fund for him. Even though the senior Mitchell thinks Ralph is a disgrace, he doesn't want his son to starve. "It wouldn't look good at all in the *Wall*

Street Journal," Ralph says. But also, Ralph clings like a limpet to a part-time job pounding the piano at a school of ballet.

In some ways Terry has the best sideline for a preclassical musician. His uncle owns Monza's, the only four-star Italian restaurant in Queens. Even without going to restaurant school, which his uncle wants him to do, Terry can always get work there. Free meals, too.

Only David gets along without other work. David is our lutenist. He's also remarkably good-looking, in a tousled, dreamy way. The combination of the lute and the little-boy-lost appeal makes David absolutely irresistible to women. This solves his economic problems. "They want to feed me and look after me," he says, "so I let them. Why not? When I get bored with one and leave, I can always hock the lute until the next one."

I'm billed as the director of this gang, and I guess I do handle most of the programming, arranging, and promoting. But when we play, there is no director. Our kind of group is like an infield in baseball. We're all the fingers of one hand, the limbs of one body, the thoughts of one brain. That is, when things are going right. When they're going wrong, the Antiqua Players is five obstreperous people arguing with each other in music.

At the immediate moment, of course, all five Antiqua Players were just plain hot.

"I want a cup of coffee," I said. The others looked at me with horror.

"He wants coffee," said Terry. "On a morning like this."

"Alan, you poor thing, we understand," Jackie said. "But we've got a five-hour drive ahead of us. . . ."

"Four," I said.

"Five," she repeated firmly. "And if we don't get the rest of our things into this station wagon and get moving, we won't get to Apple Hollow until three o'clock. And some of us *do* want to rehearse."

"Okay," I said, "I get the message. No coffee."

"No coffee until we're all loaded and ready to go." Actually, it didn't take us too long. The instruments in their cases were clumsy but not heavy. Jackie's viola da gamba was the bulkiest.

It's the size of a cello and has to ride flat on its back. David's lute never wants to fit in any car. But the smaller instruments, the music, and the music stands all load easily, and since we were only going to be away for one day, our clothes took up almost no room. By eight-thirty, we were ready to roll.

"You see?" I said, "I told you we only needed one car." And we did seem less cramped than usual.

"The legs," Jackie said.

"My God!" said Ralph. When we'd moved the harpsichord, we'd lifted it off of its supporting stretcher. We'd taken apart the stretcher and, as always, we'd carefully taped the pieces in a neat package. Just as carefully, we'd left the package on the studio floor.

Sheepishly, I made a final trip upstairs to retrieve the stretcher. When I came back, everybody was in the station wagon. I wedged the bundle in behind the rear seat and got myself behind the wheel. True to her word, Jackie handed me a cardboard cup of hot liquid. It was the unspeakable coffee the Greeks who run the pizzeria across Amsterdam Avenue brew for their enemies in an octopus tank in their back room. "Cheers," I said, taking one sip and balancing the cup on the transmission hump. I started the engine, switched on the air-conditioning, and headed north on Amsterdam. The first sound out of the radio was the Purcell "Trumpet Voluntary." We were thrilled, even though it's really by Jeremiah Clarke.

Thou Only Shalt Have Phyllis
John Dowland, To Giles Farnaby

CHAPTER TWO

"Did anybody find out anything else about Apple Hollow?" We'd left the steaming city behind and had settled down to the pleasant but monotonous drive northward through Westchester and Dutchess counties. New York public radio had faded out about ten miles back, and we hadn't yet picked up Albany. So, just to pass the time, I threw out the question.

"I asked my headmistress," Jackie said, "and she said, 'Well, I understand they're doing some *very* good things there.' I knew exactly what *that* meant."

"Ummm," said Ralph from the back seat. "A house of horror, no question. Progressive or the other thing?"

"I understand experimental," I said.

"Oh, dear," Ralph said.

"But creative," I said. This much I'd learned firsthand from the young lady who'd called to inquire about booking us.

"One of my parents heard you in Geneva," she'd said. "I think it was my mother. It might have been my stepmother. I forget. But she said you were super. Anyway, I'm Artist Liaison Person this year and I think we'd really learn a lot from having you here. And you'd probably enjoy the experience, too. There's a lot of really good creative people at Apple Hollow."

"Well, that sounds fine," I'd said.

6

"We can pay," she'd said. "It's only eight hundred dollars. But we'll give you dinner, too, if you want. Some of the kids are really good cooks."

"That's all right," I'd said hastily, "eight hundred dollars is okay. And don't bother about dinner. We never eat just before a performance."

"What about after the performance?"

"No, no, that's okay. Really, we won't feel like eating." Not school food, and especially not if the cooks were eleven or twelve years old.

I must say, though, that the Apple Hollow Artist Liaison Person—her name was Melanie and she was sixteen, not eleven—knew what she was about. Within a week after I'd sent out our performance contract, she'd sent back a signed copy. With it came a carefully marked road map and clear directions to the school, which is in the Berkshire foothills not far from Tanglewood. The countryside is beautiful. Besides, we were working on a new repertoire for three fall concerts, and I was delighted with the chance to try out some of the material on a live audience.

At about noon, we turned off the Taconic State Parkway and began working our way north and east into Massachusetts on secondary roads. We stopped at the first diner we saw, ate lunch and drove on, with Terry complaining about the quality of the jelly doughnuts, of which he'd eaten four. By two o'clock, we were at Apple Hollow.

The place really is spectacularly pretty. It's an old farmstead in a cup on a hillside, with far views across a valley. The apple trees that give it its name were heavy with the ripening fruit. Among the maples and elms at the rear of the property, the white clapboard school buildings looked snug and homelike, not at all institutional.

Even though it was still summer, the school, or some kind of school program, was in full swing. There were children everywhere, the little ones scampering and tumbling on a green lawn with brightly painted wooden playground equipment, the teenagers walking sedately along well-tended paths, tossing Frisbees back and forth or just lounging on the grass.

7

"Wow," said Jackie as we drove around slowly in search of the administration building. "Utopia."

"I wonder what it's like here in March," said Ralph.

"Don't be negative," Jackie said.

Through the trees, I caught sight of an enormous red barn. Beside it was a pond. People were in swimming. In the center of the pond was a big white wooden float with a diving board. I could almost feel the coolness of the water close around me. "This has to be it," I said prayerfully.

It was. The narrow road led straight to the barn. A door in the red siding was labeled "OFFICE." As we pulled up, the door flew open and out popped a small, sunburned, plumpish girl. She was wearing some sort of baggy garment over a damp bathing suit. Right behind her lolloped an enormous brown dog of no ascertainable breed. It was hard to say who looked friendlier, the girl or the dog.

"You're Melanie," I said.

"And you're Mr. French. I am really *thrilled* to meet you. It's so *great* you could come." This was delivered in the kind of squeaky voice you'd want your kind sister to have if you had a kid sister. Between Melanie's voice and the dog's furiously waving tail, the Apple Hollow welcome was a celebration. Furthermore, Melanie was ready for us. At her signal, a crew of youngsters appeared to help us move everything into The Room, which was what they called the place where we were to play.

The Room turned out to be a small auditorium the kids themselves had framed into one end of the vast barn. The massive wide planking of the original floor had been formed into a stage. On it, we set up the harpsichord and the rest of our gear. Surrounding us on three sides were tiers of benches, homemade out of plywood. These stretched up steeply into the gloom of what had been the hayloft. The place would have been an oven, except that two huge doors set in the end wall had been fastened open to admit daylight and a delicious breeze. Just outside, beyond a strip of lawn, was the pond.

"Is everything all right?" Melanie asked anxiously.

8

"Fine," I said, "perfect. We *can* rehearse in here this afternoon?"

"Sure, absolutely. Mr. French, could I ask you something?" she looked at me appealingly.

"Ask away."

"Could I and a couple of my friends come to the rehearsal? We'll be quiet, I promise. We'll sit way up in back and you won't even know we're there. Please?"

I looked at the others. "What about it?"

David shrugged. "Okay by me."

"Jackie?"

She was just starting to tune her gamba. Melanie was watching, fascinated. Jackie smiled at her. "Why not?"

Ralph and Terry had no objection.

"Okay, Melanie," I said, "I'll make you a deal. You let us go for a swim in your pond and you and two very quiet friends can stay in here when we rehearse."

"Oh . . . *great*," Melanie squeaked. Her face screwed up into a big grin. "Of *course* you can go swimming. I was going to invite you anyway. Do you all have swimming suits?"

We all did except Terry, and one of Melanie's moving men had a suit that fit him. Fifteen minutes later, we were all splashing in the pond. It felt wonderful.

"Come on, Alan!" Jackie called. "I'll race you to the raft!" Damn and blast the woman, she swam like a startled trout. No furious kicking, no flailing arms, and yet there she was, levering herself up on the float while I was still in the water. With what dignity I could muster, and trying hard not to pant aloud for breath, I joined her.

"Where did you learn to swim like that?" I demanded.

"My uncle's farm," she said. "Why?"

"I just wondered." One of the many things I love about Jackie is that she's a country girl, born and raised in a little Indiana town. Jackie loves to do the things country kids are supposed to do. She can sail and ride horseback and bait a fishhook and milk a cow. She'll tell you from the look of the land in winter what crops will

9

be coming up on it in spring. Being anything but a country boy myself, I find all of this fascinating. But also, I think it makes a difference. Musically, I mean. So many musicians do nothing but perform music, eat, drink, and abuse drugs. And play tennis. If I have to listen to one more second violinist tell how he and some other second violinist beat Yo Yo Ma and Peter Serkin 6-4 6-4, I think I'll lose my mind. Jackie's utterly different. She laughs at me for saying so, but I think her upbringing in the countryside adds something special to the way she plays.

I reached over and gently rubbed her bare tummy.

She grinned at me. "You can't swim as fast as I can, so you're going to overwhelm me with sex?"

"Something like that," I said.

"Well, it might work," she said. For a moment, we lay quiet, side by side on the sun-warmed wooden deck. Overhead, an occasional swallow zigged and zagged against the blue sky, doing its part to lower the insect population of Apple Hollow.

"Jackie, I said, "when are we going to get married?"

"Soon," she said. "I think I'd like to do it in the fall." She rolled over to let the sun get at her back. Then she said, "Alan . . . why don't you practice more?"

"Huh?" I said. "I *do* practice. I practice a lot. Besides . . . ."

"I know what you're going to say," Jackie said. "You play so much that you're always in practice."

"Well, it's true," I said. "Anyway, what's that got to do with getting married?"

"I don't know," Jackie said. "Nothing, I guess. But it's so wasteful. Every time we play together, I pick up something new from you about interpretation or style. I just wish . . . ."

"What?" I said.

"I don't know," Jackie said again. "I worry about you. I think you should work a lot harder on *something*. Violin, flute, anything."

"When we're married, you can reform me," I said. We both laughed, but afterward Jackie gave me a determined look.

"I'll do it," she promised. "Look. I'm not trying to be bossy. But

I think you're terrific, and I want you to *be* terrific when you play. So there."

"You're wonderful," I said. I was touched by her earnestness, and a little disturbed. "When do I start getting terrific?"

"November," she said. "Let's get married early in the month, maybe on the third or fourth, so I can get moved uptown before Thanksgiving weekend." She sighed. "It's funny. Even for you, I hate giving up that apartment." I didn't blame her. Jackie's place was only one room in a Village walkup, but it was rent-stabilized, sunlit, and as cozy as a wren's nest.

"How can I make it up to you?"

She smiled and kissed me. "No problem," she said. "New drapes in your place. A dishwasher. *And* one hour of practice together every night."

"How about two sheep instead, and my mother's second-best quilt?"

"Sorry," she said, "those are my terms."

"Ah, well. You drive a cruel bargain," I said. "I accept."

"Thank God," Jackie said. "I thought you were going to turn me down." She got up suddenly and, laughing, grabbed one of my arms with both of her hands and tumbled me into the water. As I came up, sputtering, Jackie dived in and swam to my side. Sure she meant mischief, I gulped in air. Then I grabbed her and held her close, the contact doing nothing for my self-control. For a second, she clung to me, gazing anxiously at me as if I were a new score to be memorized. "Alan," she said softly, "I love you. Do you love me?"

I nodded, my chin bobbing absurdly in the water.

"We'll be married in November?"

"Yes," I said. I let her go so I could tread water. We swam in to where the pond was only waist-deep.

"We'll live happily ever after?"

"You bet," I said.

"And we'll work very, very hard?"

I gazed at Jackie fondly. "We'll talk about it later," I said. Jackie made a cup of her two hands and squirted water at me.

11

"Duck," she said. I made quacking noises. "No, silly. In the water." Obediently, I submerged herself and waited until Jackie had planted her feet on my shoulders. Then I stood up and she did her balancing act.

"You have to promise to love, honor, and obey me," I said.

Jackie wavered back and forth, gave a little shriek and dived off me into the water. She surfaced, rubbed her eyes and tugged at her bathing suit to make sure it covered her adequately, which I'm happy to say it did not do. "I will cherish you," she said. "'Obey' is out of the question. And our practice hour is not negotiable. What time is it?"

"We'll see about cherishing, and how should I know what time it is?"

"You're our leader, aren't you? Leaders should know these things." We made our way ashore and toweled off. Ralph had already disappeared into the barn, and David and Terry put down their paddleball gear and came over to join us.

"You see?" Terry said, "no Frisbee." Ever since he'd reached for a David Brodkey power throw and torn a fingernail on his right hand, Terry had obeyed one of the few ground rules of the Antiqua Players: No Frisbee-playing within three days of a performance.

"Good for you," I said.

"I move we don't change," said David. We looked at each other.

"David," I said, "you are a genius. Go tell Ralph." A few minutes later, five half-naked but comfortable musicians were in place in the barn. I asked Melanie to switch on the stage lights. Gazing at us in wonderment, she did so. "Don't worry," I said, "it's what we call an undress rehearsal."

[T]he word 'descant' signifieth, in our tongue, the form of setting together of sundry voices or concords for producing of harmony . . .
  Thomas Morley, A Plain & Easy
    Introduction to Practical Music
    (1597)

CHAPTER THREE

By seven-fifteen, the barn was starting to fill up with people. From the door of the tiny room which served as "offstage," I was indulging in my favorite sport of counting the house. Or, rather, of trying to figure out just what sort of an audience this one would be. It was an odd mixture. There were lots of youngsters from the school. Whatever the formal education was like at Apple Hollow, the student body took its culture seriously. Mingling with the students or coming together in groups by themselves were types in tweed jackets or bib overalls who could only have been school administrators or members of the faculty. Finally, a fair number of other adults, better-dressed than the teachers but also running to beards, long hair, and wire-rimmed spectacles, seemed to me the local residents Melanie had told us about earlier. "The arties," she'd called them scornfully. "They want to be able to say they were here."

"Excuse me, Alan." Ralph pushed by me and disappeared in the direction of the lavatory. Even though we'd be on in five minutes, I made no effort to stop him. He would lock himself in one of the cubicles and would be comprehensively sick to his stomach. Stage fright always does this to him. Afterward, to keep his hands from getting too cold, he'd put on the sheepskin-lined gloves he brings with him to every performance. I've even seen him put on an

13

overcoat and a wool scarf in July. The instant the concert starts, of course, Ralph's shivering stops and he plays as if he hadn't a nerve in his body.

Three minutes. I reached into my pocket for the mouthpiece of my sopranino recorder and fitted it to the body of the instrument. Then, I stuck the whole thing under my armpit to keep it warm. I glanced around at the others. Jackie was tightening her bow. David had his lute belly-up on his lap and was straightening one of the frets. Terry had cocked his chair back against the wall. His feet were propped on another chair, his hands were folded behind his head, and he was gazing dreamily at the ceiling. Terrified, obviously.

Ralph, pale but calm, slipped back in the room and gave us a small smile. He still had his gloves on.

"We'll go on in about a minute," I said. For a summertime school concert, formal dress is obviously inappropriate. Some musicians fancy the opposite extreme of total disarray, but it's too distracting for the audience. We compromise. No designer jeans or Navaho blankets. The four male Antiqua Players wear dark slacks and white open-collar shirts. Jackie wears a long skirt— prudent, because the gamba is held between the knees—and a simple blouse.

Terry aroused himself, stretched, picked up the little drum called a tabor he was using in the first piece and joined the rest of us at the door.

"Everybody zipped up? Buttons all buttoned?" I asked brightly. Nods. "Okay, let's go."

Blinking in the bright lights and hearing a patter of applause, we filed onstage, made our bows, and took our seats. As a rule, in each half of a program we focus on one particular period or musical style. And we start off with something that shows off how we sound as an ensemble. But tonight we were experimenting. For our opener, we'd picked an *estampie*, a quick medieval French dance in three-beat rhythm, and worked it out as a solo with tabor accompaniment. If I could get it going at speed on the tiny, shrill sopranino recorder, it would start the evening with plenty of glitter.

I got to my feet and stood for a moment in silence. That caught the attention of the audience. Gradually, the noise from out front lessened, until the whole place was hushed. I caught Terry's eye as he sat relaxedly holding the tabor. He gave me a wink to show me he was ready. So was I.

Casually, almost like a kid whistling on his way home from school, I piped the first strain of the *estampie* and the first ending. As casually, Terry picked up a counter-rhythm to go with the repeat and the second ending. Quickening the tempo slightly, I moved into the second strain. Terry, grinning, followed me into the repeat. He loves the drum. By the end of the third strain, we were boiling along and the audience was getting excited.

When you play a tiny woodwind like a piccolo or a sopranino recorder, one thing you have to watch out for is taking too much breath. You don't need a lot of air to make these small instruments sound, and if you do gulp down a chestful, it just sits there in your lungs soaking up carbon dioxide from the bloodstream faster than it gives off oxygen. So, you *feel* out of breath. The trick is to breathe shallowly and regularly.

Congratulating myself on avoiding hyperventilation, I moved into the second of the three repeats of the entire piece. Terry was staying with me, backing up the whistling of the recorder with an insidious pattern of offbeats. What the hell, I thought. On the final run-through, I nodded my head up and down a couple of times to alert Terry, then speeded up the pace even more. Now, if only my fingers, all bunched together over the fingerholes of this miserable little instrument, didn't fall off. . . . They didn't, and neither did Terry's. By the end, which comes abruptly and unexpectedly as in much medieval music, we were going nearly twice as fast as we had been at the start.

Panting and very relieved, I bowed to acknowledge a small storm of applause. Terry jumped up to claim his share. We were off and running.

By the time the house lights came on again at intermission, I'd made a list of mental notes about our new material. David's lute solo was too quiet to follow my noisy opening. It would have to be scheduled later, behind the four-part Binchois dance suite. We weren't allowing enough time between numbers to switch instruments. And so on. Musically, everybody had played nicely enough. But there was plenty of rehearsal work ahead.

As we shuffled offstage after taking a couple of bows, I ran my eye over the audience. Among the chattering students and Melanie's "arties," one figure caught my attention. A tall man, slightly stooped, was standing by himself in the aisle to my right. He wore the black short-sleeved shirt and Roman collar of a minister or priest dressed for summer weather. He was sandy-haired, and he had a short, sparse beard. But from the right cheek downward onto the neck and under the collar, his face bore the raw purple indignity of a huge port-wine birthmark.

The ugly blemish alone made the man impossible to overlook. But also, he was gazing at me with an intensity that made me wonder for a moment if he wasn't in the grip of some sort of seizure. I shivered and glanced away. By the time I looked back again, the people moving in the aisle had crowded between us. I wasn't in the least sorry to lose sight of him.

The big surprise of the concert came at the start of the second half.

Back in the little "green room," we'd held our usual between-the-acts review of the way things were going. I remember saying, "Watch out for raggedy starts." Somebody else warned Terry that he should blow harder on the tenor krummhorn. The krummhorn is the medieval reed instrument that sounds like a giant kazoo, and unless you put a lot of air into it the thing does tend to go flat. But what I most remember is how relaxed we all were. It seemed so natural to go for a swim in the Apple Hollow pond and then to sit down together for an evening of music. We could almost forget we were giving a concert. We drifted onstage again as unconcernedly as if we were playing in my living room. And Jackie and Ralph proceeded to put on one of the most hair-raising performances I've ever heard.

"La Follia" is an old, old tune, perhaps as old as music itself. From Frescobaldi to Rachmaninoff, dozens of composers have had a go at writing sets of variations on it. A Frenchman named Marin Marais came up with his version in 1692. Marais's instrument was the viola da gamba, and to judge from what he did with "La Fol-lia" he must have had at least six fingers on each hand.

Jackie had been fooling around with the Marais for several years, picking it up in odd moments like knitting, then putting it aside to work on something else. I'd teased her about it, but she'd just smiled and gone on struggling with it. At some point, she'd gotten Ralph interested. A continuo part that calls for decorating the same eight measures again and again is just the kind of musical challenge he relishes.

Finally, the two of them had the thing sounding pretty good, so we put it on the program for this concert. But I was uneasy. If there's one rule in planning a program, it's to include only mate-rial well within the capacity of the player. Jackie has strong tech-nique, but some of the Marais variations are almost unplayable.

I needn't have worried.

From the opening bars, it was obvious that Jackie had her tech-nical problems licked. All the notes were there, even in the fastest passages, and she played them all sweetly, with none of the buzz and rattle you sometimes hear in gamba-playing. More to the point was what she and Ralph were doing with the music. After a few minutes, a theme-and-variations piece can start to sound dull and can go on being duller and duller until the audience falls asleep. Jackie and Ralph never let boredom set it. They gave every new variation its own special highlighting. As they moved into the third variation, in the wavering dotted rhythms of a French *courante,* I could see Jackie's fingers tighten slightly on the bow. *Relax, relax,* I said to myself, *loosen up.* As if in answer to my unspoken wish, her hand relaxed and her bowing remained easy.

They played the fourth, quick variation with almost mis-chievous delight in their own virtuosity. The delight was catch-ing. After one bit of bravura passage-work, I saw and heard a dignified old lady in the audience actually giggle out loud with pleasure.

Best of all, they let the music build up to its natural climax. This comes in the ninth variation, a finger-breaker that features huge skips from bass to treble and knotty ornamented phrases in between. Again, I found myself muttering silently. *Slow down,*

Ralph. Let it breathe. Just in time, they took something off the tempo, and the tiny, almost imperceptible hint of stridency that I'd begun to hear died away. Jackie's hands, those beautiful long-fingered hands I'd held so often, resumed their steady, even work on bow and fingerboard. And the slowing down let both of them avoid the frenzied head-shaking and arm-heaving that makes some performances look so awful, like sessions of electroshock therapy.

The final variations glided serenely by. I sat still and prayed that no frayed fret or breaking string would shatter the spell. The final note sounded, then slid into silence. I hear wonderful music every day of my life, and yet I hated to hear this music come to an end.

The Barn was no Carnegie Hall. But that audience, bless its heart, made noise enough to fill ten Carnegie Halls. People wouldn't stop applauding. I saw my friend the giggling lady clap her hands until she was tired, stop clapping for a few moments to rest, and then start up all over again. The Apple Hollow kids, of course, went crazy. In the midst of the uproar, David sat perfectly still. A tiny smile was on his face, and two enormous tears were wet on his cheeks. Terry was shaking his head from side to side, his lips moving soundlessly and articulating, I was certain, the single syllable, "Wow!"

Jackie and Ralph, too, sat still. For a long moment, they gazed at each other from the soul, as two people will gaze when they've done something together that has tested and taxed everything in them. I watched them. I wasn't jealous: how could I be? But I do remember thinking, with a stab of regret, that the old easygoing Antiqua Players, having hatched its swans, would soon be no more.

How we got through the rest of the program, I'm not sure. One of the numbers was another French piece, a Leclair violin sonata that I was trying for the first time on the Baroque flute. A one-keyed wooden flute is not the easiest instrument to play in tune. I recall dropping one clinker, a high C on the repeat of the first section that came out utterly, disgracefully flat. Jackie and Ralph were supplying the continuo accompaniment. Jackie's eyebrows went up and the corners of her mouth twitched as she suppressed a smile. But the silken sound she was coaxing from her gamba that night just kept carrying my feeble solo along.

At last, after two encores, we stopped playing and the audience stopped begging us for more. For what seemed like an hour, we all stood around in that little offstage cubby, waiting for the house to clear so we could pack up. Melanie joined us there, breathless with thanks and enthusiasm and bringing with her our check. But Melanie's crew had vanished, so everybody except Jackie had to help get the harpsichord off of its legs, out of The Barn, and back into the station wagon. By the time we were through, a lovely moon, nearly full, had risen over the valley, and the cicadas were tuning up their own continuo. Tired as we were, we all stood for a moment watching and listening.

"I don't know about the rest of you," I said finally, "but I'm tired. Also half-starved. But . . . ."

"Hey, Jackie," Terry said, "you played great. Both of you."

"Definitely," David agreed. "It was definitely one of those moments."

"And what does Alan French think?" asked Ralph.

"Alan French wants to hug you both," I said. "You were absolutely wonderful."

"*Christus,*" Jackie said. "Let's go now, while we're still ahead."

We piled into the station wagon and drove away from Apple Hollow, heading south toward dinner. And home.

[I]t will be a great absurdity to use a sad harmony to a merry matter or a merry harmony to a sad, lamentable, or tragical ditty.

Thomas Morley, p. 290

CHAPTER FOUR

Those winding country roads, so charming by daylight, are no fun at night, even with a bright moon to boost your headlights. I was glad to get us down out of the hills and onto a nice, straight state road, and happier still when a lighted signpost announced that we were approaching the Quarry Hill Inn, Septimus Spode, Prop.

There were still cars in the parking lot. "Kitchen's open," Terry grunted as we turned in past the inn entrance. "He'll serve us."

"What makes you so sure?" I asked. Terry, as befitted an expert, disdained to answer me.

"He'll get about nine-fifty for an entree, salad, and beverage," he said. "Dinner, the five of us, run you sixty-five, seventy bucks."

"That's ridiculous," Jackie said.

"Maybe so," I said, "but we're stopping anyway."

"We can celebrate," David said.

"Celebrate what?" asked Jackie. Spending more than twenty dollars in a restaurant strikes her as immoral.

"Celebrate your and Ralph's great performance," I said. "Come on. I've got some cash and the Apple Hollow check."

"I'll buy the wine," Ralph said.

The decor was a little heavy on hunting prints and carefully shined brass harness fittings. But Septimus Spode turned out to be

20

an expatriate New Yorker, in a red, red vest with silver buttons, who had fond memories of the far East Eighties, where he'd lived for years. "How wonderful!" he exclaimed when we told him we were musicians, and on the strength of his wonder he stood us a bottle of perfectly drinkable red wine.

When we opened our menus, I started to laugh. Shish kebab— "Dinner on a Dagger" was its billing—was nine-fifty. Bay scallops, nine-fifty. *Boeuf en croute,* ditto. Veal, you guessed it. Steak was more and chicken was less. But everything else except a ham and swiss on rye cost exactly nine dollars and fifty cents.

"Never doubt me," Terry said.

"Okay, maestro," said Jackie, "what should I eat?"

"Take the chicken," Terry said.

"How come the chicken?" I asked.

"The other stuff is frozen for sure," Terry said. "Who cooks *boeuf en croute* to order in the boonies?"

"How about the scallops?" David asked.

"Take the chicken. Maybe the veal. *Maybe.*"

"Jackie?" I queried as the waiter padded over.

"My spirit is broken. The chicken."

"I want a steak," Ralph said suddenly.

"Oh, Ralph . . . " Jackie began.

"I'll pay the extra," Ralph said hastily. By this time, we were all a little lightheaded.

"Four chickens, one steak," I told the waiter.

"Yes, sir." He scribbled on his pad.

"Wait a minute," said Terry.

"Sir?"

"I'll have the scallops."

"You fink," I said. Everybody laughed. I said to the waiter, "You'd better bring us some white wine."

"You have to drive," Jackie said.

"Listen," I said. "Tonight, you are ravishingly beautiful. Also, and without a doubt, you are turning into one of the finest string players in the world. Right before the eyes of your friends and associates. We all love you. We all respect you. Now . . . will you stop being Den Mother?"

21

Jackie blushed. "I'm sorry, Alan, I really am."

"Besides," I grumbled, "you may be one of the finest string players in the world. But I still say that in the fourth variation you should play the first triplet on three up-bows. Dah, dah, dah. That way, they come out nice and mechanical."

"How?" Jackie asked.

"Dah, dah, dah," I repeated, picking up a fork and moving it like a gamba bow.

"That sounds *too* mechanical," Jackie said. "You've knocked over the salt."

"Well, think about it," I said.

"She's right," Ralph said.

"I think it should be up-*down*-up," David said, "dah-*dah*-dah."

The waiter brought the white wine. I drowned my sorrows in a glass. "Another thing," I said. "Ralph's trills are getting too fast."

"You're out of your tree," Terry said.

"That's just what anybody *would* say who conned everybody into chicken so he could get the scallops," I said.

"Now, now," Jackie said soothingly. "Dinner will be here in a minute."

"You know," Ralph said thoughtfully, "I think he may be right. It's where you trill," he said to Jackie, "and I answer." The two of them got deep into a conference on trills. They were still at it when the waiter came with dinner. Finally, with the food on the table, I grabbed the fork again and used it to tap a signal on the side of my wine glass.

"Ladies and gentlemen," I said, "dinner is served. The technical discussion will now cease."

"Hedonist," Ralph said, reaching for his own fork.

Jackie smiled deliciously at me. "Now who's being Den Mother?" she asked.

"I am," I said. "I'm famished. I'm also tired, and we've still got a three-hour drive ahead of us. *And* some of us have to play tomorrow. So, let's eat."

Frozen or not, the food tasted good and we did it justice. By the time we'd munched our way through to Deep Dish Country Apple Pie With Fresh Vermont Cheddar Chunks and cups of coffee, we

22

were all feeling relaxed and happy. Septimus Spode himself reappeared with a bowl of afterdinner mints, and we talked about New York for a while. Septimus suggested brandy, which the others accepted and I dutifully turned down. The brandy made people relax even more.

"Ah," Terry sighed. "That hit the old spot." He loosened his belt. "You know, I keep thinking about that tour we made in seventy-six."

"That's right," Jackie said, "I remember. The Hartford Greyhound Terminal. We had dinner there before the Conservatory concert."

"Jesus," I said, "I'd nearly forgotten. I *want* to forget." We all laughed. But it's true, we all do want to forget the more horrible aspects of touring. The leaden cheeseburgers at the campus restaurants. The lumpy motel beds or, worse, the uneasy hospitality of the luckless faculty members who volunteer—or are drafted—to serve as hosts to visiting musicians.

"Why do we do it?" asked Ralph.

"Aw, come on," said Terry, "you know it's fun."

"Maybe for you," I said, "but I'm getting too old to fit in bus seats."

"What you're really getting," Jackie said severely, "is too fat. It's time you went on a diet. You'll never fit into your tuxedo in time for the Saint Cecelia concert."

"Sure I will," I said rashly.

"Well, you'd better cut down. You know what happens if you have to play the flute and your pants are too tight."

"There's nothing wrong with being fat," said David, just to keep the argument alive. "Sometimes I like being fat."

"Come on, folks," I said. "Jackie, you're making me feel guilty. David, you're making me feel stupid for feeling guilty and for not having a brandy." I waved a hand at the waiter, who came over with the check. "Let me see," I said. "What's five times nine-fifty?"

"Forty-seven-fifty," said Terry instantly. "Your tip oughta be about seven bucks. Give the guy fifty-five dollars."

23

"We've been here about two hours," Jackie said. "It costs about fifty cents a minute."

"I'll ignore that," I said. I fished two twenties, a ten, and a five out of my wallet and reminded myself that it was time to renew my library card. Also to buy myself a new wallet.

The way out of the dining-room led us past the doorway of a dimly lighted bar. As we filed by, a man seated at the bar suddenly rose and came toward us. Even before he put a hand on my arm to stop me, my alarm bells were going off and the sirens were beginning to whistle.

It was the man I'd seen at the concert. The one with the port-wine birthmark.

"It's Mr. French isn't it? Mr. Alan French?" The man, for all his unprepossessing appearance, spoke pleasantly enough in an educated British voice.

"What is it?" I said sharply. I'm enough of a New Yorker to dislike being approached too closely by strangers. This man, in his black clerical shirt and trousers, was standing directly in front of me and only a foot or two away.

"As a matter of fact," he said politely, his tone in obvious contrast to my own, "it's something rather interesting."

"Alan, are you coming?" Jackie called from the restaurant doorway.

"Just a second," I called back. "Sorry," I said to the man, "you'll have to excuse me." I pulled my arm free of his grip and tried to step past him.

"Oh, please," he said. Behind the sandy beard and the birthmark, his face was young and stiff with embarrassment. His eyes, I saw with surprise, were almost frightened. "Please. Speak with me for just one minute. I've come such a long way to find you. Father sent me, you see. Sit inside with me, you and your friends."

"Some problem, Alan?" Terry turned back to find out what was keeping me. The others trailed him a few steps behind.

"I don't know," I said.

"Look here," said the young Englishman. "I only want a moment of your time. I must speak with you. It's frightfully urgent."

"Life and death, no doubt," Ralph said.

24

"Well, not that, no," the young man said, flushing. "But important. I promise you, it will take only a moment."

"Weren't you at our concert tonight?" I asked him.

"Yes, yes, I was. Very good you were, too. Marvelous, in fact. I can see why Father wants me to find you." He looked around at all of us. "I say," he went on, "could we possibly sit down?"

I caught Jackie's eye.

"You're the one who wanted to get started back," she said. But she was curious. We all were.

"Okay," I said to the young man, "why not?"

The Englishman led the way into the deserted barroom. We all took chairs around a scarred old table. As if by magic, Septimus Spode materialized. He took orders for beer all around except for Jackie, who hates beer. She had a second cup of coffee instead.

"Now," I said when we'd been served, "what's this all about?"

"First of all," Ralph chimed in, "who are you?"

"Right," the young man said briskly. "I'm Brother Martin Oswald. I belong to a smallish religious order, R. C. of course, the Oratorians of Saint Loy."

"R. C.?" I asked.

"Roman Catholic," Jackie said.

"Right," Brother Martin said again. "You won't have heard of us. We're contemplatives. Mostly, that is."

"You mean, you sit around and think about God?" asked David.

"That's it," said Brother Martin. "I mean, we do other things, too. We farm, make cheese, ale, the lot. And we chant the liturgy quite a bit. But we're not really out in the world the way the Franciscans are."

"How big are you?" asked Terry. I remembered, he has a cousin who's a nun.

The young man looked embarrassed. "Well, actually, not very," he said. "There are about forty of us."

"That's not bad," said Terry.

"Well, we've lost quite a few," said Brother Martin, "but one must expect that, mustn't one, given the state of the world?" He took a sip of his beer.

"Fair enough," I said. "But now, what exactly do the—"

25

"Oratorians," supplied Brother Martin.

"—the Oratorians of Saint Loy want with us?"

"Ah, well," Brother Martin said, "that's a bit complicated. That's going to take some time to explain. In actual fact, Father wants to handle that aspect of the situation in person."

"Who is this 'Father' you keep referring to?" I asked him.

He looked surprised. "Didn't I say?" he said. "No? Oh, well, it's Father Valentine Gilmary, our superior. He's a wonderful man, quite astonishing, really. He sent me down to the concert with instructions to make contact with you. 'Follow them, if you have to,' he said. 'But don't you come back here until you've had a chat with them.' Well, of course, he had to say that. I'm so terribly shy, you understand, because of this." He touched the purple blotch on his face. "Father had to give me a direct order."

This time, it was Jackie who asked the question. "But what does Father Gilmary want?"

Brother Martin sipped some more of his beer. "I'm only his secretary," he said, "and I don't *know* exactly what he wants. He doesn't tell us everything, I assure you. 'Brother,' he said to me once, 'I believe in keeping things separate.'"

"But you must have some idea," said Jackie.

Brother Martin looked sideways at her, then looked away. "I *think*, now, mind you, I don't know," he said, "Father wants to make you a kind of business proposition."

"Oh, no," said Ralph, "not again." The others groaned.

"We're musicians, not businessmen," I said. "The last time we got involved with a businessman, we wound up in a lot of trouble." I didn't elaborate, and nobody else did, either.

"Father Gilmary's not a businessman," said Brother Martin a shade indignantly. His glass was nearly empty. I wigwagged to Septimus, behind the bar, to bring him another beer. "Ta," Brother Martin said, taking a sip from the fresh glass. "Now, do be reasonable. I can't tell you what Father has in mind, except that he wants to meet you. 'Brother,' he said, 'tell Mr. French to come see me. Better still, bring him back with you.'"

"Back where?" I asked.

"Oh, just up the hill a bit." Brother Martin gestured vaguely at

26

the leaded-glass casement Septimus had had installed in the bar. "We're staying at the Recollects' motherhouse. They've been *very* kind. Super, really."

"Wait a minute," I said, struggling to keep up. "Your Father Gilmary's got some sort of deal he wants to talk over. So he sends you down to get hold of us and bring me back with you? Is that it?"

"Bang-on," said Brother Martin.

"Unreal," David said.

"I think so, too," I said. Terry, I noticed, was yawning. "Look, Brother Martin," I said, "the best thing to do is to have Father Gilmary . . . ."

"He said you'd say that," said Brother Martin triumphantly.

"Say what?" I said. "I haven't even finished my sentence yet."

"Father said you'd say, 'Have Father Gilmary ring me up.' He said to tell you that it's much too important to discuss over the telephone. That since you were in the district anyway, why waste time and money driving all the way back? 'Tell him,' Father said—"

"All right," I said, annoyed. "That's it. We're going." I pushed back my chair.

Brother Martin seemed stunned. He made no effort to get up. "He said you'd never forgive yourself," he muttered at the table.

"He said *what*?" I said.

"Personally and professionally." He didn't throw out the line the way a salesman would, just to get me to react. On the contrary, Brother Martin sat still with his head down. His fingers toyed with the beer glass, tilting it and turning it around and around on the table in front of him. If it was salesmanship, it was cleverly handled. And, confound the man, it was working.

I turned to Jackie. "What do you think?"

"It's nearly eleven," she said. "If we're going to get back in time to get any sleep, we'd better start now." She paused. "And you'd better get started up the hill, wherever that is."

"You think I should go?"

Jackie drew a deep breath. "No. But I know *you*. You're dying to find out what this is all about. So, go ahead. We'll take our car. Only . . . call me later."

"Hey, Jackie," Terry cut in. "You think this is safe?"

Brother Martin gave a nervous laugh. "My dear chap," he said, "we're really not villains, you know. We'll take excellent care of the lad and get him back to you by morning."

I gave the car keys to Ralph and we all walked out to the parking lot. Terry and David climbed in the back of the station wagon. I opened the right front door for Jackie. She got in and held up her face for a kiss. "Listen," she said, "behave yourself. And don't sign anything."

"I'll call you in a couple of hours," I promised. Ralph started the car and I watched its tail lights disappear down the highway.

"She's lovely," breathed Brother Martin in what seemed to me a highly unsacerdotal way. He might have been reading my thoughts, because he added hurriedly, "Not to worry, Mr. French. But one can't help noticing, can one?"

"I suppose not," I said.

We stood for a moment listening as the sound of the car died away and the small noises of the August night reasserted themselves. I was tired. Probably, I should have gone back with the others. Then, this whole ridiculous episode would be over and done with. But it was a beautiful night, and even though I was feeling foolish, I admit I felt exhilarated to be setting out on a midnight frisk.

"Brother Martin," I said expansively, "take me to your leader."

*I call that the noble manner of singing, which is
used without tying a mans self to the ordinary measure
of time . . .*

Caccini, Le Nuove Musiche

CHAPTER FIVE

Brother Martin's car was an ancient yellow Volkswagen that belonged to his hosts, the Recollects of St. Anthony. Shy and monkish he may have been, but once behind the wheel he drove uphill toward our destination with the mad zest of a steeplechase jockey. Never having set foot in a monastery before, I wondered out loud what this one would be like if we got there alive. Brother Martin laughed. "You'll love it," he promised. He flung the protesting Volkswagen into a sharp left turn up a gravel driveway. Tall oaks and maples lined either side of the drive, but beyond them I could see open space in the moonlight. The monastery, it seemed, was surrounded by an enormous sloping lawn. "Quite right," Brother Martin said. "Golf course. Rich chap had it built for his own amusement. Left it to the Recollects. Clubhouse, too. That's where they live."

"The Recollects play *golf?*"

Brother Martin giggled. "No, no, no, good God! Though now you mention it, it might be rather funny to watch Father Anselm have a go."

At the end of the driveway was a sprawling brick-and-stone mansion that could well have been a clubhouse. Equally, it could have been a millionaire's private home. We left the car in a graveled parking area occupied by only one other vehicle, a battered pickup. It had a rosary looped over the rear-view mirror. We could have used one too, I thought. The gravel scrunched under our feet as we made out way up to the front door.

Brother Martin caught hold of the massive iron door-knocker and slammed it several times against the plate on the door. It made a tremendous, reverberating racket. I winced. "Aren't people asleep?" I asked.

"Oh, no, not too many," Brother Martin said. "Most of them will still be in front of the telly at this hour."

We waited for several minutes in silence. Then, very faintly, I could hear the shuffling of footsteps on the far side of the heavy door. A burglar-chain rattled, a key squealed in the lock, and the door swung slowly inward. "Hello there, Brother Simon," Brother Martin said.

"It's you, is it?" said a guarded voice. "Come on in, Brother, and you too, Mister—"

"French," I said.

"You, too, Mister French." The voice gave a dry cackle. When I stepped inside, I could see that the voice belonged to a tiny, stooped old man. Like Brother Martin, Brother Simon was clothed in a short-sleeved clerical shirt and slacks. But on his feet Brother Simon wore ancient bedroom slippers of maroon leather. The suspenders that would normally hold up the slacks hung loosely. Obviously, we'd disturbed Brother Simon's rest. "That's okay, Mr. French," he said when I apologized. "I'm used to it. It's what you get when you keep house for a bunch of night-crawlers. Know what night-crawlers are, Mr. French?" he asked me.

"Fishing worms, aren't they?" I said. Whatever I'd expected of my very first monastery, it wasn't this. Brother Simon cackled again.

"Some are and some aren't," he said cryptically. He turned away to shuffle back down the long slate-floored hallway. "Some are and some aren't," he muttered to himself. Just as he was about to disappear into a room at the end of the hall, he called to us, "Father What'sit's up in the library, waiting for you. You'd better get on up there. I'll bring you tea."

The main staircase led upward to our left, into a world of shadows. Halfway up, a single bulb gleamed reluctantly in a fixture meant to hold three bulbs. A setting for *Wuthering Heights.* Whatever the Recollects of St. Anthony had done when they'd taken over the place, they hadn't altered the decor. As we turned the corner of the first-floor landing, something glittered at us from the gloom. When I saw what it was, I laughed nervously. It was the glass eye from a huge moose-head mounted high on the dark, paneled wall.

Our footsteps sounded hollowly along the corridor. "You mustn't mind Brother Simon," Brother Martin said cheerfully. If the haunted-house atmosphere bothered him, he didn't show it. "He's been here donkey's years looking after the place and he's got a bit funny. But he's all right, really. Heart of gold, that sort of thing." I made the noncommittal noise you make when people say things like that about other people. I wasn't at all sure about Brother Simon's heart of gold. More and more, I wondered why I'd let the others go back to New York without me.

"Here we are." Brother Martin pushed open a leather-bound swinging door. He ushered me into a room that smelled delightfully of old books in old bindings, not so delightfully of damp and mildew. This room, at least, was decently lighted by a couple of big floor lamps and by one of those nice old green-shaded brass reading lights that antique dealers will sometimes sell you for too much money.

The brass lamp stood on a massive mahogany table. The man getting up from behind the table was obviously the man I'd been brought here to meet. "Hello," he said in a deep, pleasant voice. "I'm Father Gilmary, your kidnapper."

"Hello," I said back. We shook hands briefly. Inappropriate as the phrase may be, I thought to myself, you, my friend, are a handsome devil. Father Gilmary had the square-chinned, rugged face of a Marlborough Country cowboy. Dark hair grew low on his forehead. His eyes were deep-set, intelligent, and vividly green. His smile of greeting revealed very regular, very white teeth. Yet I didn't find Father Gilmary's good looks off-putting. For one thing, although of course I couldn't be sure, he seemed relatively unself-conscious about them. For another, from the lines etched into his

31

face and deeply carved around his mouth, Father Gilmary looked to me like a tired, troubled man.

"I expect you'd like to be told what this is all about." He advanced easily to stand facing me in the center of the room.

"Well—" I began.

"Of course. But, er, just for the record, you *are* Alan French, aren't you? The musician?"

"That's who I am," I said.

"And it's true that you're rather a specialist in early music?"

"True enough."

Father Gilmary thrust his hands into the pockets of his black clerical jacket and stood still, eyeing me keenly. After several seconds, he gave a little nod of his head, as if he'd made up his mind about something, and smiled. He had an extraordinarily charming smile. "That's all right, then," he said. "I'd expected somebody perhaps a bit older. But this is splendid. You'll do splendidly."

"Do for what?" I asked.

Father Gilmary turned to Brother Martin, who was standing by the library door. "Brother, you've done a good night's work. I don't mind telling you that." Brother Martin flushed with pleasure. Automatically, he put up a hand to the blemish on his face. He muttered something incoherent. "Bear with us for just a moment, Brother Martin," Father Gilmary smiled again, "while I put our guest in the picture."

Without waiting for a reply, Father Gilmary strode quickly to the far end of the library. He picked up something fairly sizeable from a low table and returned with it. He needed both hands to carry it, and when he drew nearer I could see why. The thing he had gone to fetch was a steel box. It was about the size of a Manhattan telephone directory, and it must have weighed a good ten pounds.

Father Gilmary set the box carefully on the big table. From his pocket, he took a key-ring. He selected a flat steel key and inserted it in the keyhole set in the lid of the box. He turned the key smoothly, once, then twice, and withdrew it. When he lifted the lid, a side of the box opened on hinges, like a safe-deposit box, to give easy access to what was inside. As Father Gilmary reached in,

I could see that the box was lined and padded with thick bottle-green velvet.

The steel box held a book.

Its binding was of leather dyed a beautiful deep blue and richly stamped with an allover pattern of flowers in gold. The flowers seemed familiar, and a second glance told me why. They were *fleurs-de-lis*. Another design was stamped on the spine of the book, but I couldn't get a look at the detail.

"This is what we've brought you here to see," said Father Gilmary.

He slid the book clear of its container, reached over and handed it to me. For all of its thickness, it was surprisingly light.

"Very pretty," I said. "What is it?"

"Before I tell you that," said Father Gilmary slowly, "I'd like you to have a bit of a look-see at it yourself. No! no!" he added sharply as I started to open it. "Not like that! You might break the spine!"

"Sorry," I said.

"Great Heavens! Sit down first, man, sit down!" He pulled up a chair to the big table and slid aside the steel casket to give me more room. "Lay it flat. That's better, that's the ticket. Now, open."

Music.

As I turned the pages, they rustled softly. The old paper—Father Gilmary told me later that they made it out of silk rags—whispered under my hands as if it had secrets it wanted to confide. But this isn't the music I mean. The real music was there on page after page, laboriously written out in an ink that time had turned the brown of autumn leaves. Exquisitely written, in a hand both delicate and strong. By modern standards the notes were crowded close together, their stems crooked, their tails quick light pen-strokes. Yet, even at a glance they were decipherable. As I read, skipping from page to page, the music began to come to life. Pavannes, galliards, allemagnes, corantos, voltas, a jig or two—dance pieces, all for keyboard. A whole group of fancies or fantasias, the parts not in vertical arrangement but set down one after another: descant, treble, altus, quintus, tenor, bassus. Then, airs

33

for voice and viols. Mixed in with all of this were pieces written not in staff notation but in the tablature, or musical shorthand, used for lute music.

Some of the pieces were familiar, or carried familiar names: Byrd, Tallis, Giles Farnaby, Robert Johnson, John Dowland. Others were nameless. Many were new to me. Nearly all of them, even the simple ones, would be beautiful.

"Well, now," said Father Gilmary as I glanced up from the pages of manuscript. "What do you make of that?"

"It's obviously someone's personal music-book," I said. "That is, if it's authentic."

"It is authentic, I assure you." Father Gilmary got up from his perch on the edge of the table and walked around it to sit across from me in his own big chair. "The question is, whose music-book?"

"Does it matter?" I asked, "because, musically—"

"It matters," Father Gilmary interrupted. "It matters very much indeed."

"Why?" I wanted to know. "Francis Tregian owned the *Fitzwilliam Virginal Book*. The pieces are copied in his own hand. But nobody except a few scholars cares who *he* was. What's important is the music."

Father Gilmary tilted himself back in his chair. He made a little tent of his fingers and sat silently for a long time, tapping index finger against index finger. I thought for a moment he was doing hand exercises for the flute. Then he said, "Look here. Did you happen to notice the very first page?"

"No," I said. "Frankly, I was too interested in the music."

"Have a look now," commanded Father Gilmary. Obediently, I shut the book and reopened it at the beginning. A couple of blank pages were bound in first, as protection for the manuscript itself. Then came the initial manuscript sheet. It was worn and yellowed and bore not music but a written inscription. The ink was faded, and I was tired. I had to squint hard to make out the words.

"Eli-za. . . ."

"Yes?" said Father Gilmary.

"'Eliza-beth her boke of Musike,'" I read very slowly. "'If thou a musician a Judge shalbe/Pric nott thy notis in the lyne of peruer-site.'" Then something in Latin. "'Semper eadem.'"

"'Always the same,'" Father Gilmary translated. "Have you any notion whose motto that was?" The U. S. Marines? No, dummy, that was *semper paratus*.

"I have no idea," I said.

"She got it from Lady Tyrwhit," said Father Gilmary.

"Who did?"

"She was sixteen and not in a very good frame of mind," he went on as if I hadn't spoken. "She had been playing the lute and the virginals for about eight years."

Light dawned slowly.

"You're trying to tell me," I said incredulously, "that this book belonged to—"

"Precisely so," said Father Gilmary. "The private musical note-book of Queen Elizabeth the First. Begun when she was a young girl and kept up for the rest of her life. Well, not quite. But until she was, er, elderly."

"But how," I began. "I mean—"

"You mean, if this thing is genuine—"

"Right," I said. I was beginning to catch his habit of interrupt-ing. "If it's genuine, then how do you happen to have it?"

"Oh, we've had it from the beginning," Father Gilmary said.

"The beginning?"

"Well, from the end, I should say. Of her reign, that is."

"I see," I said. "Picked it up off the stereo in the throne room."

"You're not too far wrong, at that," said Father Gilmary with a short chuckle. "We got it—it was given us—on the day the Queen died."

"Given to you," I repeated stupidly.

"By one of the Queen's ladies-in-waiting who was one of Us."

"He means, who was a secret Roman Catholic," Brother Martin put in from his armchair by the door.

As he spoke, there came a noise from the corridor outside. It sounded as if someone was clacking two blocks of wood together. Loudly and with gusto, like a four-year-old in an infants' rhythm class.

35

"Good God," I said, "what's that?"

Before anybody had time to answer, the library door was flung wide open. If Brother Martin hadn't ducked, disaster might have followed. Instead, in marched old Brother Simon. Replacing the bedroom slippers on his bony bare feet were wooden clogs with canvas tops. These, obviously, were the noisemakers. In his hands, Brother Simon carried a large tin tray. On it were balanced three enamel mugs with chipped blue rims, full of steaming liquid, a cut-glass bowl holding paper packets of sugar and sweetener, half a box of paper napkins, and a plate with an assemblage of Oreo cookies.

"I brought you your tea," Brother Simon announced unnecessarily. His voice was loud enough to wake the dead. His little black eyes sparkled with pleasure and malice. "We're out of the good tea," he added happily. "I had to use the White Rose tea bags." Just in time, I snatched the Queen's music-book out of the way, as Brother Simon banged the tray down on the table hard enough to slop tea over the paper napkins. "Enjoy your treat, in Christ's name."

Father Gilmary closed his eyes in momentary agony, but all he said was, "Thank you, Brother."

On his way out, Brother Simon paused. "I'm going to bed," he said. "You'll have to wash up yourselves. I can't be waiting up for you all night." He shut the door behind him, not quite slamming it. The sound of his clogs echoed in the hallway. If any of the other people in the place had managed to sleep through the proceedings thus far, his exit would have had them wide awake and trembling. How did they stand it? I wondered.

"Tea?" Father Gilmary spoke as calmly as if nothing unusual had happened. He handed me one of the mugs. It was so hot I nearly dropped it on the polished mahogany. "Sugar?" With blistered fingers, I finally managed to get some of the sugar out of one of the little envelopes into the tea. "*And* biscuits." When I shook my head, Father Gilmary helped himself to a handful of Oreos and handed the plate to Brother Martin, who followed suit. The two of them munched away like schoolboys. "Excellent!" Father Gilmary brushed away a crumb and sat back in his chair. "Now," he said, "let's get down to business."

36

I can give you no general rule but that you must
have a care to . . . avoid standing in unisons.
                                Thomas Morley, p. 270

CHAPTER SIX

"But that's utterly fantastic," said Jackie.

"Me, too," Ralph said, holding out his cup. I poured them both fresh coffee and topped off my own third cup of the day. Brother Martin had dropped me at my door at four o'clock that morning, which is no time to have to face Amsterdam Avenue. At ten-thirty, with two afternoon lessons and a late rehearsal scheduled, I needed the caffeine. I also needed, and wasn't getting, moral support.

"It's what I deserve for staying late in the country," I said. "But still. . . ."

"You mean, you really believe this story about the book being Queen Elizabeth's music-book?"

"Jackie, I don't know," I said. "I only glanced at it. The music is remarkable." Jackie snorted.

"The deal is remarkable, too," Ralph said.

"What deal?" David and Terry came in together through the double glass doors.

"Get some coffee, you two, and sit down," Jackie said. "You're never going to believe this. Alan, tell them."

"Okay, but stop prejudicing them. Nobody believed Galileo, either." I told them about the drive up to the monastery and about meeting Father Gilmary. I told them about the music-book.

37

And then I told them about the proposition Father Gilmary had offered me over the White Rose tea and Oreos. "They say they can prove the book really did belong to Queen Elizabeth. They've got documents. They say they think some of the pieces were written by Queen Elizabeth herself."

"Copied, you mean," said David.

"*Written.* Composed."

"Terrific," Terry said. "You got any Danish?"

"In the white paper bag," I said. "The brown bag is crullers."

"So what's the deal?" Terry asked through a mouthful of Danish.

"If the book is what Father Gilmary says it is, it's worth a fortune, right?"

"It could be," David said cautiously.

"Especially if it proves that Elizabeth the Protestant Queen was really pro-Catholic."

"Catholic, schmatholic," said Terry. "Give us the deal."

"Shame on you," I said reproachfully, "after all those years in the choir at Our Lady of Mount Carmel."

"Hey, listen," said Terry, "watch that or I'll get my cousin after you."

"His parole officer will be mad," David said.

"Okay," I said. "Father Gilmary's religious order, which is broke, wants to sell this book."

"No *way*," said Terry at once.

"Of course not," I said. "They're looking for a million bucks. Maybe more. *But* . . . if we come up with some money, they will sell us the exclusive performing rights to the music in the book. Also, the exclusive publishing rights in the U. S. A. for one year. The idea is that we do a program, concertize, do a record, and all of this is great advance publicity for *them* when they put the book on the market."

There was a long silence.

"How much money?" asked David.

"Have some more coffee," I said to him. Everybody laughed. David eyed me warily. "The good news, maestro," he said.

"Ten thousand dollars," I said. Everybody laughed again. Except David. David looked interested.

"You've seen this book, actually seen it?" he asked.

"Sure thing," I said.

"What did you think?"

I drew a deep breath. "I thought it was real."

"What do you mean, 'real'?" David asked.

"Real Elizabethan," I said. "Whether Elizabeth herself was the owner, God knows. But I held the book in my hands and it felt right."

"Oh, Alan," Jackie said reproachfully.

"You weren't there," I said, but David cut me short.

"Wait a minute, Jackie," he said. "Let's just work this thing out." He turned back to me. "Okay. This Father Gil-what's-his-name. Is he legit?"

"He certainly looked the part," I said, "and those others, Brother Martin and the old man, Brother Simon, well, you saw Brother Martin. I thought they looked all right, too."

"Give me the name of their order," said Terry, "we can check them out."

"How?" asked Jackie.

"My cousin," Terry said.

"The one who's on parole?" Ralph asked politely.

"Nah, another one. This one's a pastor in Sunnyside. They've got directories."

"Brother Martin told me the name," I said. And miraculously, the name popped into my mind. "Oratorians. The Oratorians of Saint Loy."

"Let me write it down," Terry said, scrawling on a sheet of music paper.

"O-R-A . . ." I spelled it out. "Now. Suppose Father Gilmary does check out. Then what?"

David smiled. "Then, we go ahead and make the deal."

"*Christus*," Jackie said. "Another one of us is crazy."

"Excuse me, I have to leave," said Ralph. "I've got a twelve o'-

clock at the barn." The barn was the very good ballet school where Ralph worked as a *répetiteur*.

"They can wait a couple of minutes," I said. "David, what have you got in your wicked little mind?"

David's smile broadened. "Whether this thing is for real or not, you know, that's not *our* problem. That's *their* problem. It's up to them to prove the book is what they say. All we have to do is the music. The worst that happens, we wind up with a good record, a couple of good concerts, a bunch of publicity for *us*."

"Yeah, really," said Terry. "The only thing is, what about this ten thousand dollars?"

"I've been thinking about that," David said.

"And?" said Ralph.

"What if we don't have to come up with it in cash?"

There was a pause while we all thought about not giving Father Gilmary ten thousand dollars in cash.

"It's an idea," I said.

"I mean," David said, "suppose we went to Father What's-It and said, 'We'll give you your ten thousand dollars, only not in advance. We'll give it to you later, out of the money we make on the concerts and recording.'"

"Why wouldn't Father Gilmary just smile politely and go right across the street to James Weede?" asked Ralph.

"What a dreadful thought," said Jackie. James Weede is one of our competitors. He's a big, blond guy with a bushy beard. He rules over a group called the James Weede Consorte. Politeness forbids me to tell you what we think of James Weede and his Consorte. We can forgive his putting his performers in costume: tights and parti-colored tunics for medieval concerts, powdered wigs and breeches for what he calls his "Esterhazy Experiences." We can forgive his unpleasant habit of adding bells, wood blocks, cymbals and other noisemakers to early music, and of making every repeat louder and faster than the one before. What we can't forgive—at least, I can't—is that the James Weede Consorte is ragged, out of tune and just plain dull.

"I don't think Father Gilmary would fall for James," I said. "Besides, there's a lot of music for virginals in that music-book, and Weede doesn't have a regular harpsichordist."

"That's right, appeal to my vanity," said Ralph. But I noticed that he was making no move to get up and leave for the barn.

"He could get one, though," Jackie said.

"Right now, Father Gilmary probably doesn't even know that James Weede exists," I reminded her. "Let's get back on the track. David, have you got any money?"

"Nope," said David.

"Ralph, have you?"

"I don't think so, Alan. Not for this."

"But you *would* play? If we made the deal, I mean."

"Absolutely," Ralph said. "Why not?"

"I've got a couple of grand," Terry said suddenly.

"*You* do?" I said.

"You know it," Terry said. "From Monza's. Tips. And I know where to get more."

"Where?"

"Don't ask, Alan," Ralph said quickly. We laughed. Terry shot us an injured look.

"Get off of my case," he said. "It's nothing like that. My uncle, he likes me, is all. Last time I was out there working, he said to me, 'Terenzio, you ever need money for something good, you let me know.'"

"Maybe we'd better hold your uncle in reserve," I said. Terry shrugged.

"Fine by me," he said.

"Jackie?"

"Only my dowry," she said stiffly. Then, she softened. "But if you guys all insist on going out of your minds, I'll cash in Aunt Lucy's savings bond."

"You're wringing our hearts," I said. "How much?"

"Five hundred dollars. And not one penny more."

"*Awright!*" Terry bounced out of his chair and gave Jackie a hug.

"Okay," I said. "I'll put up another twenty-five hundred," Al-

41

most the last of the money from Europe. "With five thousand in all, we should be able to deal. If not, let him go to James the Weede."

In the end, the thing was fairly easy. Terry called his cousin the pastor in Sunnyside, who called his friend the Bishop of Rockville Centre. What His Excellency did I don't know, but in about a week a letter arrived with a very fancy coat-of-arms on the envelope. It told us that the Oratorians of Saint Loy, or Eloy, were indeed a legitimate Roman Catholic religious order and that Father Valentine Gilmary, O.S.L., was its Vicar General. "That means he can sign checks," Terry explained.

I had to make quite a number of phone calls to the small Massachusetts town that was home to the Recollects of Saint Anthony. The Recollects had only the one extension. So, I got used to Brother Simon's jeering, grumbling voice and to the endless waits while he shuffled off to find Father Gilmary. Father Gilmary wasn't too surprised by our response. Naturally, I started out low. When I told him over the telephone that we were prepared to advance three thousand dollars in cash for the recording and performing rights, there was a long, long hush and my heart skipped a beat. But then I heard him give a little sigh, as if he'd been expecting something like this. "There are other musical groups, you know," he reproved gently. I did know, I told him, but I assumed he's already done some screening. He laughed. "You're too clever for a simple priest, Alan," he said. "Suppose we settle on five thousand?"

"Make it four," I said. Father Gilmary sighed again.

"Four, and you pay the solicitor's fees."

"It's a deal," I said.

Nobody looks less like a solicitor than our lawyer. Instead of black broadcloth, Mickey Weintraub wears rather vivid Brioni stripings. Instead of chambers in the Middle Temple, Mickey occupies a tiny office high up in the Brill Building. How he concentrates on legal matters with enthusiastic rock groups auditioning all around him, I have no idea. But Mickey knows everything there is to know about the intangible legal rights surrounding a piece of music and its performance. Give him a deal to "structure," as he puts it, and the loose ends won't unravel unless you want them to.

And so, one warm, sunny day toward the end of September, I drove my rented car up the hill to the Recollects' monastery, braved Brother Simon and his demanding refreshments, and came away with a signed contract and an armload of photocopies of music. Queen Elizabeth's minstrels were getting ready to do their number.

CHAPTER SEVEN

All of a sudden, we were frantically busy.

Our contract with Father Gilmary gave us until December 15 to get ready for our first concert of the music in the book. By then, the advance publicity about the book would be whetting the public's appetite and drumming up interest among would-be buyers. We'd have no trouble filling even a big hall.

So, we had two and a half months to transcribe what was in those photostats into playable arrangements, to pick out the ones we wanted to play, to organize a program, and to rehearse. Meanwhile, there were our three other concerts, one in October, two in November. Plus all of our private commitments, from giving music lessons to playing one-night jobs around town.

"Don't worry, we'll do it," I told the others. But I wasn't sure how.

There were sixty-one pieces in the music-book. I bought a ream of music paper, a box of Number Two pencils, a red rubber eraser, and a giant bottle of aspirin, and on the first of October, a miserable rainy day, I started transcribing the first piece. It went by the inspiring title "Ut Re Mi." The syllables stand for the first three notes of the C-major scale. The music consisted entirely of repetitions of the same three notes. Slow repetitions, quick repetitions, plain repetitions, embroidered repetitions. It was not subtle music.

44

The piece was a kind of warm-up piece for virginals, the curious name the Elizabethans gave the small, rectangular harpsichord. In fact, it sounded like a sonata for doorbell chimes.

The hell with it. I tossed my pencil onto the worktable. Naturally, it bounced once on its eraser tip and rolled off the table onto the floor. And naturally, when I leaned over to pick it up, I banged my head on the edge of the table. "Goddammit!" I said aloud. Just then, in walked Jackie, the rain still sparkling in her dark hair and dripping off the plastic of her gamba case onto my one half-decent Turkish carpet.

"Goddam *what?*" she asked brightly. I rubbed my head.

"Take a look at this stuff," I said. "It's awful."

"Now, now," Jackie said. She came up behind me and leaned over my shoulder to look at the photostat. I could smell a trace of her perfume. "Well," she said after a minute, "it's not too interesting, I agree. But just keep going. I'll get us some coffee." She gave me a quick kiss, eluded my seeking hands, and headed for the kitchen.

On the strength of her promise, I retrieved the pencil and started on the sixteenth "Ut Re Mi" variation. It was no more exciting than the first fifteen, but at least it was the last.

The next piece was entitled "Ut Mi Re." I uttered a lusty Elizabethan oath and asked myself, not for the first time, why I hadn't gone to medical school. Jackie came in with the coffee. She handed me a cup and I took one sip and, for the first time, the morning started to make sense. "Jackie," I said, "why does my coffee always taste like mud and why didn't I go to medical school?" Jackie laughed. She was sitting with her long legs curled under her on the battered sofa, sharing it with piles of music, the morning's unopened mail, and the Baroque oboe I had decided to master. She looked so bright and unmarked that the sight of her made me faintly dizzy.

"Your coffee always tastes like mud because you insist on throwing a handful of coffee into a pot of water and letting it sit there until it turns into, well, mud—"

"I clarify it with an eggshell," I said defensively.

"—and the thought of you as a doctor is enough to make me

45

sue the A.M.A. for malpractice. But I love you anyway." She put down her coffee mug decisively. "I can only stay a minute, Alan. I've got to get out to Farmingville. But I'll be back for rehearsal tonight." The school where Jackie teaches is in Farmingville, a town out on Long Island. She goes there twice a week. It's a long commute, and Jackie could easily find work closer to New York, but she won't change. The job and the steady money it brings in are Jackie's security blanket.

"Okay," I said, "but before you go, take a look at some of this." I held onto "Ut Mi Re" and handed over the rest of the stack of photostats. For a few moments, we were quiet as Jackie leafed through them. I was just finishing the third "Ut Mi Re" division, to use the Elizabethan term for a variation, when Jackie said, "Look, Alan! There's writing in the margin of this one."

"Which one?" I asked. When I'd handled the book itself, up at the monastery, I'd noticed that several of the pages bore inscriptions. But I hadn't had enough time to try to decipher any of them.

"It's a galliard, and I can't read what it says. Can you?" I shoved a stack of recorder music out of the way and sat down next to her. A galliard, or galiardo, is a dance in triple time—three beats to the measure—that usually follows either the slow, stately pavanne or the less slow, less stately allemande. I put my arm around Jackie's shoulders and tried to concentrate on the uneven gray lettering of the photocopy.

"Hold it closer to the light, okay?" I squinted at it. Squinted harder. "It says . . . 'E-li-za . . . her galiar-do . . . writte a Hatfyld . . . anno 1550.'"

"Eliza her galiardo," repeated Jackie, "written at Hatfield anno 1550. Oh, Alan! Do you think it could really be by her?"

"Who knows?" I said absently. I was reading the music. "It sure is a pretty one, though." I looked up. Jackie's face was flushed. Her lips were parted with excitement. "Hey!" I said. "You were the one who was so skeptical about this thing, remember?"

"But Alan," she said. "I didn't know there was anything like this in the book! I'll bet that's her handwriting!"

I gave her a squeeze. "You really are an incurable romantic, aren't you?" I said. "Except about me." She sat forward quickly, freeing herself from my arm, and looked indignant.

"You," she said loftily, "are not the Virgin Queen."

"I admit it," I said.

"So, why should I be romantic about you? Besides, your handwriting is even worse than hers."

"Stop putting me on the defensive," I said. "If you give me ten minutes, during which time you dry off your gamba and tune it, I'll do an arrangement of Eliza's galiardo, just treble and bass, and we'll see what it sounds like."

"Great!" Jackie jumped to her feet, then leaned over and kissed me warmly. "I *am* romantic about you, Alan, really. Do a *nice* arrangement."

"Right," I said, "one with heavy emphasis on the bass part and plenty of skips and passage-work for the bass instrument, in this case the viola da gamba."

"I knew you'd understand," she said.

I moved back to the worktable and began scribbling out some music. The galliard followed the usual pattern of galliards for keyboard or lute. That is, it had three sections, or strains, each one echoed by an elaborate, ornamented variation. If you were a so-so player, you'd play just the undecorated strains. If you were better than that, you'd play strain one and its fanciful repeat, then go on to strain two and its repeat and so on.

As I worked, I was dimly aware of some musical scrapings in the background. Jackie, tuning her gamba. The sounds died away. She was ready. Another five minutes, and so was I. "Here," I said, handing her a couple of pages of music manuscript. "Can you read it?"

"Barely," she said. She set the pages on her music stand, clipping them in place with spring clothespins so they wouldn't sag or fall off, the way they always do for me.

"Got an A?" She had an A. Quickly, I tuned my treble viol and kicked a chair into place next to hers. Jackie was right. I must do something about my musical handwriting. It's awful. "I'll give you one for free," I said, the bow poised in my hand. She nodded.

47

"One and two and three and . . . " we were away smoothly into the music.

All I'd done was transcribe the bass and treble lines and sketch in the in-between harmony. For anything more elaborate, we needed a whole consort of instruments—or else the lute or virginals, on which the player can fill in the chords. But this much was enough to make us realize that if the first Elizabeth of England had written what we were playing, she was a musician of considerable talent. Don't misunderstand. We weren't breathless in the presence of mighty genius. A pleasing galliard is not a grand-scale masterwork. But "Eliza's Galiardo" had a nice lilt to it, a folk-tune quality that made it fun to play. And the variations, which in bad Elizabethan music are often just boring runs up and down the scale, were deftly handled. The third one even had some interplay between bass and treble. Jackie would ask, I'd answer, she'd ask again, I'd respond, that sort of thing. By the time we reached the final note, we were both smiling with pleasure.

"Hey," I said.

"It's lovely," she agreed. "Let's do it again."

"For sure. Ready? One and two and three and. . . ."

Exactly on the beat, the telephone rang.

"Hell," I said. I stood up, put down the viol and bow and went across the room to answer the hateful thing.

"If it's David," Jackie said, "tell him he's got to be here on time."

"Is this Mr. Alan French?" It wasn't David. It was a woman's voice, one I'd never heard before.

"Speaking," I said.

"One moment, please, Mr. French, for Tarleton Morlock." Tarleton Morlock? My eyebrows did a disappearing act into my hairline. Tarleton Morlock was *the* splashy name in the New York art world. At twenty-six, when he was still studying at the N.Y.U. Institute of Fine Arts, he had plucked from the attic of a half-ruined country mansion in Ireland a dusty painting in a warped frame. What happened next the newspapers never quite managed to explain. But Morlock got his find out of the country, and when he and the painting appeared in New York, the painting turned

48

out to be Giorgione's *Meleager Overtaking Atalanta*, a rarity missing since 1787 from the collection of the kings of France and forgotten even by the experts. The discovery, and Morlock's yarn of how he'd tracked it down, earned him both TV talk-show acclaim and a blue-chip scholarly reputation. The gossip was that, at thirty, he'd turned down the directorship of the Metropolitan Museum of Art on the ground that he couldn't afford it, a piece of audacity that had the Met trustees gasping like so many winded joggers. Whether or not that tale was true, mention any serious piece of art business and Morlock's name was sure to pop up. Once or twice, at big New York culture bashes, I'd seen his handsome, bold face and tall dome of a head close at hand. But in the realm of the arts, I was a peasant and Morlock was a prince. As far as I knew, he'd never spared me a glance.

So, what the hell did he want with me now?

"Mr. French. Hi! Tarl Morlock!" The husky voice, familiar from so many TV interviews, was full of geniality and warmth. And self-assurance.

"Who is it?" asked Jackie. I made a face at her to keep quiet.

"Hi," I said, I hoped casually, into the receiver.

"You know, I've always loved your work," Morlock went on. "The Antiqua Players, that's the name of your group, isn't it? I thought so. Well, your stuff is terrific."

What do you say, dear? "You're very kind," I muttered.

"People like us ought to know one another," Morlock said easily. "But you know how dumb life is in this city. There's never any *time*."

"No, there isn't," I said humbly.

"Well, let's make some. Do you think you could bear to lunch with me this Friday?" He issued the invitation in the deprecatory style of a celebrity whose invitations are seldom refused. A charmer, Mr. Morlock, no doubt about it.

"I'd be happy to have lunch with you," I said, "but can I ask you—"

"No, no," Morlock said authoritatively, "don't ask me a thing. Not now. Just come to the house. You know, eight-eighteen Park. Come about noon. We'll eat and then we'll chat."

49

"Well, but—"

"That's fine, then. See you Friday. And for God's sake don't dress." The phone banged down on Morlock's final command. I hung up, too, and took a second to draw a deep, deep breath.

"What on earth was that all about?" Jackie demanded. She was still seated behind the music stand, ready to play.

"You're never going to believe this," I said.

"Believe what?"

"That, my dear girl, was none other than Tarleton Morlock."

"Alan, you're kidding," breathed Jackie.

"Honest injun," I said, "and he wants me to have lunch with him on Friday."

"Tarleton Morlock wants you to have lunch—oh, Alan, it's the music-book, of course. It must be."

"Of course it is," I said irritably. "But what I don't understand is how he knows about it. Father Gilmary wasn't going to break the story until November fifteenth, and we certainly haven't told anybody."

Jackie glanced at her wristwatch. "*Christus*, look at the time. I've got to catch my train." Swiftly, she began to pack up her gamba. "I'll be back about seven," she said.

"Good," I said. "Everybody's supposed to be here by eight. We have to go over the Morley. Otherwise, catastrophe. What do you want for dinner?" Jackie eyed me warily.

"No more Venetian eggs," she said firmly. Venetian eggs were what happened when I decided to surprise her with scrambled eggs, frozen spinach, and tomato sauce.

"I'll think of something," I said.

"That's what I'm afraid of." I held her coat as she wriggled into it. Then, for one tender moment, I held her. "Darling."

She kissed the tip of my nose. "You've got to find out what Morlock wants," she said. "But I'm not pretending I like it."

"Why not?" I said.

"I know you. You'll go in there with the most awful chip on your shoulder, looking for trouble."

50

"Not me," I said. Jackie lugged her gamba to the front door. I held the door open for her.

"You get right back to work on that music," she said, "and leave the arts alone."

"Stay dry, Eliza," I called out. But the elevator door was clanking shut, so I doubt if she heard me.

I declare that I bow before the merits of others, and that I respect the value of every one.
Girolamo Frescobaldi, Toccatas (Rome, 1614), Preface to Vol. I

CHAPTER EIGHT

There's a brand of furniture polish that comes scented with lavender and a dash of lemon. I forget the name, but it comes in a tin from England and you're supposed to use it on your fine antique furniture. At eight-eighteen Park Avenue, which is a corner building on the west side of Park in the low, low Seventies, they employ this furniture polish on the paneling of the elevator. They also employ a human being, not a self-service mechanism, to make the elevator go up and down. At eight-eighteen Park Avenue, I said to myself as I was ferried smoothly skyward, the super probably doesn't have to operate a second-hand tire business out of the basement.

I was, of course, not in the least impressed by my surroundings. Why should I be? My shoes were shined, my hair was brushed, my blue blazer had all of its sleeve buttons, and my tie was centered neatly in my shirt collar. I had every right to be riding in a walnut-lined elevator that smelled discreetly of Old English Lavender furniture paste.

"Morlock," the elevator man sang out as he brought the car to a careful stop.

I stepped out, the elevator went away and I was left alone in the foyer of the Morlock apartment. Standing on the black and white marble checkerboarding that's more or less standard in apartments like this one and gazing straight at the doorways that led to the rooms beyond. Something was odd about this setup, but for a moment I couldn't figure out what. Then, I realized. There was no outer door. No massive steel-framed barricade, complete with peephole, police lock, and snarling German shepherd separated Tarleton Morlock and his riches from the world outside.

The foyer was quiet and almost empty. There was no art in sight. Only a small table stood sedately against one wall, its polished surface mirroring a beautifully shaped white porcelain bowl full of fresh chrysanthemums.

For a second, I stood bemused, wondering what to do. Then came the sound of footsteps and Morlock himself appeared in a doorway. In shirt-sleeves, his cuffs turned back to reveal freckled, muscular forearms, he was living up to his well-publicized reputation for informality.

He let loose a volley of cordiality. "Well, for God's sake! Alan French in person! Come in! So glad you could make it!" He gave my hand a brief dry squeeze and ushered me through the door and down a hall. Inside the apartment, there was plenty of art. I caught glimpses of several paintings I would have loved to look at more closely, but Morlock swept me along as if we were on some urgent errand. "You've got to see this!" he kept saying, "it just arrived this morning. Timing couldn't have been better."

A few paces more brought us to another doorway. "My study," Morlock said. "Place is a mess, it always is. But what the hell, come in anyway." It looked neat enough to me. Bright light poured in through the French windows along the far wall, but the room was so huge that its corners were in shadow. Over a couch at one end of the room hung a tapestry. Some woven gentry in feathered hats were assaulting a leopard with bows and arrows. The leopard looked surprisingly cheerful. The tapestry must have been at least fifteen feet square, but it didn't look too large for the wall it was on. Not at all.

Morlock steered us to a table. "Here we go," he said. On the table lay a violin-case. Morlock's hands were quick and efficient unsnapping the locks. "It just got here," he said again, "just in time for you."

53

"Very considerate of it," I said.

"It's a Balestrieri, of course," Morlock said, unruffled. "Probably the father. Care to try it?" He gave me a sideways look and a lantern-jawed grin that said, I dare you. It struck me then that Tarleton Morlock the esthete might just be a very tough cookie.

"Why not?" I picked up the violin, plinked the strings for tuning, tightened the bow, and nestled the instrument under my chin. It felt wonderful. When I played two or three measures of Sarasate, it sounded even more wonderful. Discipline, Alan, I told myself. I put down violin and bow and nodded my thanks. "It's always fun to play a super fiddle."

"Yes, I can see that it would be," Morlock said. "This one's going straight down to Tampa. They're paying a zillion dollars for it. They'll keep it in the museum and lend it out to guest artists. Too bad it won't be played more often, but . . . hell, at least it's safe. Thank you for letting me hear it. I've never sold a violin before in my life, and of course I don't play myself. Used to know 'Chopsticks' pretty well, but that's about all." He gave the unabashed laugh nonmusicians often give when they confess that they're nonmusical. "Well, so much for that." Briskly, he closed up the violin-case. Then, he grinned again and said, with a gesture of his chin, "Drinks are over there. Get us both a sherry, why don't you, while I put this thing away, and after that we'll have some lunch."

Inviting a stranger to do the honors at your own bar is flattery at its most silken. Like not having a front door to your apartment, it's an expression also of great self-confidence. As I fussed with tiny glasses and Morlock's Brooks & Co. *fino palma*, my antennae were twitching to catch more of his signals. But there were none. Or rather, everything was a signal.

Morlock went away with the violin. I couldn't help noticing how lightly he moved for a big man. When he came back, we sat on the couch and sipped our sherries and he talked. He told a fascinating story about dating a Dutch painting from the metalwork the artist had painted on the lid of the lute-case in the picture. "The detective work was terrific fun," he said, "but the best fun was backing my own hand." This meant persuading a panel of experts—"those *bloody* people," Morlock called them—to admit that he was right about the date while they were dead wrong. "By God, it took a week of telling them. But they saw the light."

As I listened, the beautiful room was broadcasting exactly what its owner wanted me to feel. From twelve stories below, the mundane sound of traffic came to us very faintly indeed. The autumn sun gleamed on the freshly waxed parquet flooring and picked out the reds and blues and tawny golds of the magnificent old carpet. Everything looked and felt well-worn and lovingly handled. In one corner, a painted wood sculpture, nearly life-sized, bowed its austere head as if in homage to Morlock's authority.

"Santa Barbara," I said in recognition. "Wasn't she the patron saint of artillery?"

"Well, well," Morlock sounded surprised. "Not bad. Damned few art historians know that. Of course, damned few art historians know *anything*. She's not Spanish, of course." He nodded at the sculpture. "Probably German, possibly Danish, certainly late sixteenth century. She's sweet. I may keep her for a while. But yesterday I got a marvelous offer from Houston."

"How can you bear to part with her?"

He gave me a cold smile. "One thing you learn in this business, my friend, or you don't stay in business very long, is to turn over your inventory." He looked at me to be sure I was getting the message. "So . . . everything must go. Although I admit I'll feel a pang when my Barbie-doll goes."

"Your *what?*"

"Oh, yes," Morlock caroled, "make no mistake on that score." And he was off again, on a brilliant five-minute lecture on the origins of sculpture in the secret desires of men to give birth to beautiful, compliant women. I can't remember it all, but he ranged from the Venus of Willendorf to the mystery cults to the Mona Lisa and ended up in twentieth-century New York.

In that room, amid those wonderful old things, Morlock's big frame and long face lent a lot of force to the things he said. He might have been a Renaissance cardinal holding forth on the nature of his favorite sin. It was a captivating performance. What's more, Morlock knew exactly how and when to cut it short. Suddenly, in mid-sentence, he said, "But you don't want to know about these things." He gave his crocodile grin. "Sometimes I get carried away." He looked at his watch. "And my guests die of starvation. Finish your sherry and we'll see if lunch isn't ready."

Lunch *was* ready, on the terrace, with a canopy spread to keep the sun at bay. I knew there was a Mrs. Morlock, and small Morlocks as well, but she and they were nowhere in evidence. Alone, the two of us ate fish poached in wine and served with a delicate white sauce. We drank a Rhine wine, flowery but not sweet, and disconcertingly strong. The food was superlative. Morlock ate and drank sparingly, but I enjoyed every mouthful.

Finally, the maid poured Kona coffee into translucent china, bobbed and smiled and disappeared. And then, Morlock got down to brass tacks. "My dear friend," he said, "I have gone to some trouble to present myself to you."

"You have indeed," I murmured.

"The reason is simple. You have something I want. Oh, please—" he waved a hand to forestall any denial "—you have in your possession an Elizabethan manuscript containing music, some of it original, and believed to have belonged to Queen Elizabeth herself. I want it. Not for me personally, I hasten to add, but for a buyer. Frankly, I don't believe a word of that nonsense about its being the queen's. But it sounds of the period. If it *is* genuine, and if it *is* Elizabethan, I'll give you a damned good price for it. Even though the manuscript market is as soft as mayonnaise right now.

"Well, then, Alan, what do you say to that?" Morlock leaned back comfortably, hands clasped lightly in front of his chest and waited with pleasure for me to react to his bombshell. He looked altogether formidable.

"You wouldn't believe me, I suppose, if I told you I didn't have any such manuscript?"

Morlock laughed out loud. "I would not. My information is that you have it. And so . . . you have it. Where it came from, I have no idea and couldn't care less. Why you acquired it is a question of your motivation. Again, I couldn't care less. All I do care about is that a fairly valuable manuscript has come into your hands. Let me repeat, *fairly* valuable. We're not talking about a Shakespeare autograph. But this, er, acquisition, whether you know it or not, leaves you with some serious problems. Luckily for you, and I mean it, I want the manuscript and am prepared to pay you well for it."

There's no doubt at all that this was the point at which I should have risen to my feet, thanked Morlock for a delicious lunch, and run for home. But I couldn't bring myself to do it, I just couldn't. I was too curious. And Morlock was too much of a challenge. He had me irritated, which of course is exactly what he wanted. "What problems?" I asked him.

Again, he gave a bark of laughter.

"My dear fellow, the very fact that you ask the question shows me how serious they are. Let me enumerate." He held up a well-kept hand and, as he talked, ticked off his points on his fingers. "One, maintenance. Are you keeping your manuscript under climate-controlled conditions? No, I thought not. Is it exposed to direct sunlight? You don't remember. How about dust?" He never gave me a chance to answer. "Number Two," he said, sitting upright and pursing his lips, "there's the question of security. You're probably keeping this thing right in your flat. You're on the West Side, I suppose?" I nodded. He nodded back. "Well, let me tell you something. If it's there when you get home, you're lucky." He paused to let this sink in, then gave his harsh laugh. "Not to threaten," he said, "but when any grocery boy, any *maid* . . . You do have an alarm system? Smoke detectors? Lobby guards?" When I shook my head to all of these, Morlock looked somber. "See here," he said, "I'm afraid I'm going to have to sound terribly rude. But you do have problems, don't you? I tell you frankly that you'll be a lot more comfortable selling." He tented his fingertips and surveyed me judiciously over them. "Why, you could very easily be killed." He didn't sound as if the possibility worried him much. "And how silly to be killed for something that's probably not worth more than six or seven thousand dollars."

For a long moment, I sat there dumbstruck. Morlock's voice carried so much conviction that he almost had me convinced that I *did* own Eliza's virginals book. I was just wondering where to put the burglar-alarm sensors and how to protect myself against mur-

57

derous assault by a manuscript-snatching delivery boy when reality set in. I would have said something to break the spell, but Morlock headed me off, sure from my silence that he really had me persuaded.

"Well," he said in business-like tones, "clearly the appropriate thing is for me to have a look at your manuscript. I'm afraid it can't be today, but I could probably stop by sometime tomorrow." The "probably" was a nice touch: I liked it. "The morning would be better," Morlock added. He waited expectantly, his fingertips still pressed lightly together, his eyes on mine. The man's physical presence was overbearing, his arrogance as rank as the smell of a carnivore. He really did make me want to wrinkle my nose and move away. But there was something awesome about Morlock's self-assurance. Even in music, which has its share of egomaniacs, you rarely see anything like it.

I was uneasy about crossing him. One reason was Father Gilmary. I had no manuscript to sell, but Father Gilmary did. Morlock, as repellent as he was, was a likely customer. The other reason I was reluctant to antagonize Tarleton Morlock was more immediate. I was afraid of what Tarleton Morlock might do to me in return. Still, it wouldn't do to give in.

"I'm sorry," I said quite truthfully. "I'll have to call you."

For an instant, Morlock's eyes glittered and the muscles around his mouth worked in a fit of pure fury. I had denied him something, and I would pay. But as quickly as it appeared, the expression vanished and he was smiling. Well, you could call it a smile. "You do that," he said. "I must warn you," he added after a second, "I'm leaving in a week for Florence and Madrid. So there isn't all that much time. But do call. It would be frightful if something happened to your treasure. And it could, you know. So easily."

I'll never forget what happened next. Morlock took a sip of coffee. Then, casually, almost gleefully, he reached up and flipped his exquisite demitasse cup over the terrace railing.

A pig of a man, and a pig's gesture.

Before I could react, he was on his feet, still smiling, enjoying my discomfiture. "So nice to see you," he said. "Most interesting."

58

Still appalled, I got up, too, and let him lead me indoors and through the hallway to the antechamber. I'm not embarrassed to admit that my knees were trembling slightly. Morlock pressed the button for the elevator. "Forgive me for not waiting," he said. "There's a call I must make." To my enormous relief, he slewed around on his heel and disappeared.

*The fewer parts your song is, of the more exquisite
should your descant be and of most choice chords . . .*
    Thomas Morley, p. 145

CHAPTER NINE

It was nearly two o'clock when I paid off the cab from Morlock's and hurried across the sidewalk to take refuge in my somewhat shabbier lair. Ramón the super had appointed his other cousin Innocente relief doorman. My arrival interrupted his nap. He tilted down the chair he had leaned back against the wall by the lobby door, eased his peaked cap back so he could see me, and gave me a friendly leer.

"Wow, Mister French, it must be great being a musician," he said as I started to heave open the lobby door. "That's some chick just went up to your place."

"What chick?" Jackie wasn't due back from Farmingville until at least seven, and I wasn't expecting anybody else. Innocente's leer broadened.

"I dunno, I never see her before," he said. "She said you were going give her a lesson. So, I let her up."

"You didn't let her in, did you?" All I could think of was Morlock's heavy-handed warnings. Maybe the chick, whoever she was, was waiting for me with a knife. Innocente first looked surprised, then sheepish.

"Lemme tell you, Mister French, a dynamite looking lady like this, she'll never hurt you. You mean, you don't know her?"

"You *did* let her in," I said.

60

"I did, yes," he said with dignity. "I was sure she was no problem."

"It is a problem," I said. "You know you're not supposed to—" I gave up. "Look," I sighed, "I'm going up. If I don't buzz down inside of five minutes, call the cops."

"The *cops*? For a beautiful chick like that?" Innocente shook his head incredulously.

"Call the Fire Department, then," I said. "I don't care who you call, but find out what the hell's going on." Innocente laughed out loud.

"Okay," he said, "I call the Fire Department for you." He thought I was being richly funny. He was still laughing as I headed for the elevator.

All I wanted to do was to get inside my apartment, change into jeans and sneakers, sit down until Morlock's wine wore off, and then maybe do some practicing. Practicing clears the mind. What I did not want was some beginning recorder or flute pupil, dynamite-looking or not, cluttering up the place and making horrible noises at me. Besides, it's true that I sometimes lose the bits of paper I jot down appointments on. But I was sure I'd kept this whole afternoon clear, and for the life of me I couldn't remember telling anybody to come by for a lesson.

Such were my thoughts when I stuck my key in the lock and opened the door. They vanished instantly when I saw what awaited me inside.

She had one of those perfect oval faces you sometimes see in fashion photographs. Only, hers wasn't made up or in any other sense readied for display. It belonged to her and to nobody else. Her dark hair was drawn back from her forehead and held in place with a simple band. In her ears were tiny gold earrings. She sat quietly in her chair as I came into the room. The poise of her whole body in repose was far more disturbing than any gesture could have been. I caught the tang of a discreet perfume.

"I've been waiting for you," she said. Her voice held the faintest hint of a foreign accent, I wasn't sure of what kind. "My name is Angelica Lederman." She stopped. I guess she was waiting for me to say something, but I was so busy taking in every square

61

centimeter of Angelica Lederman that I passed up my cue. "You *are* Alan French, aren't you?" she said finally.

"Absolutely," I said. "Why?" Angelica Lederman looked serious for a moment, as if she were considering my ridiculous response on its merits. Then, the corners of her mouth moved deliciously in a small smile.

"I want you to give me a music lesson," she said. "Won't that do?"

"Absolutely," I said again. I tried to keep my tone as cool as her own. "What instrument do you play?" Again, Angelica looked at me seriously. And again, she smiled. This time, the smile seemed a bit mischievous.

"In B.A.—I'm from Buenos Aires, you understand—I played the guitar. A little. So . . . how about a lesson on the guitar?" Now, this did sound odd. Most people, when they come for a first lesson, are more definite than that. They say, I want to learn the recorder or the flute or whatever. But I do teach guitar, even though I don't play it well. And if Miss Lederman, or Miz or Senhora, wanted a guitar lesson, who was I to object?

"All right," I said. "Just for the record, I charge thirty dollars an hour."

"I will pay it. Now or later?"

"Later is fine," I said. "Do you have an instrument with you?" Angelica tilted her head slightly and smiled.

"No, I don't," she said, "I'm sorry."

"No problem," I said. "I have one we can use. Just let me get it. And if you don't mind, I'd like to change out of these clothes. Tell you what," I gestured at the pile of collapsed music stands in one corner, "while I'm changing, why don't you set up a stand?"

The guitar was in a closet down the hall from my bedroom. I remembered to buzz down to tell Innocente not to call the Fire Department. Then, I grabbed the guitar and ducked into the bedroom itself to shed my party clothes. I hung up the blazer, stripped off my tie and shirt and kept going. I was down to my briefs and reaching for a pair of jeans when I heard a faint noise behind me. I turned. There in the doorway, watching, was Angelica Lederman. She was posed like a little girl, with one knee slightly bent

62

and her hands clasped behind her. The effect was not in the least childish.

"You have a very erotic back," Angelica said.

"I do?" I said cleverly.

"Come over here," she said. On my bare feet, I padded across the room toward her. I was feeling very silly and very aroused. Angelica gazed up at me. Her eyes, set deep under beautifully shaped brows, were a dangerous dark green. Automatically, my arms went around her. She kissed me lightly, then not so lightly. With the second kiss, her lids drooped and the green eyes shut almost all the way.

"I thought you wanted a guitar lesson," I said.

"I thought so, too," she whispered. She let the tips of her fingers work on the back of my neck. Her discreet perfume wasn't so discreet after all. Suddenly, she ran a sharp nail down my back.

"Ow!" I said. Angelica moved in my arms.

"You don't like to be hurt?" she said. "Not even a tiny bit?"

"Not me," I said. And I wasn't much liking this seduction scene, either. "You have a very erotic back *and* front," I said to Angelica, gently disengaging her arms from around my neck, "but I really think—"

"You mustn't think," Angelica said. But the trouble was, I *was* thinking. About Jackie, naturally, but also about Tarleton Morlock and his harsh warnings that were really threats in drag. The combination was enough to kill my fit of amorousness dead.

"Let's stop while we still can," I said lamely.

Angelica didn't say a word.

I turned away from her and went back to the closet for my jeans and a shirt. I felt like a fool. "Okay," I said when I was dressed. "Let's start this thing all over again. Do you still want a guitar lesson?"

Angelica smiled slightly. "No, not really."

"Well, then," I said, "how about a cup of tea? Very strengthening after what you've been through."

This time, Angelica laughed. "Damn you, Alan French, I'd love a cup of tea." So we went into the kitchen. I put on the

63

kettle, made tea-bag tea for two, and we sat in the studio and sipped it together.

"This isn't exactly why I came," Angelica said.

"What, to have tea?"

"No, the other thing."

"All right," I said. "Why exactly did you come?" I watched her face take on its serious, almost scholarly, look as she sorted through a choice of answers. It was an amazingly beautiful face, and she kept it under excellent control. With a face like that, you can say almost anything.

"I came about the manuscript," Angelica said.

"About what?" I said.

"Your manuscript."

One thing was certain. I had been right to let Morlock cool my ardor. Out loud, I said, "What do you mean?"

"I knew you had an Elizabethan manuscript," Angelica said, "and I wanted to see it."

"Why?" I asked bluntly. Angelica stared at me out of the amazing green eyes.

"To find out if it was authentic, of course," she said. "I'm a trained bibliographer. My field is Renaissance manuscripts." My face must have registered my disbelief, because the trace of a flush darkened her cheekbones. "Don't look so surprised," she said reprovingly, "it's perfectly true. Or maybe you would care to see my diploma from the Bibliothèque Nationale?"

"That's all right," I said, "but tell me. Suppose you did get to look at the manuscript and it was genuine. What would you do?"

"We'd pay you a lot of money for it," she said.

"How much?" Angelica looked amused.

"It all depends on what I find out," she said. "But maybe a lot."

Just to have something to say while I collected my thoughts, I asked, "Who's this 'we' with all the money?"

Angelica smiled coolly. She was back in control and enjoying it.

"The people I represent. They are substantial people."

"But their identity is a closely guarded secret, I suppose."

"I promise my clients absolute confidentiality, yes."

"I see." I was beginning to think out a strategy. "You come to my apartment and lie your way in past the doorman. You wait for me and tell me you want me to give you a music lesson. You then decide to give *me* a lesson in something else. Now you tell me you're a big expert in Renaissance manuscripts and some sort of a dealer, and some people you represent will pay me a lot of money for something you think I own."

"If it's genuine," said Angelica.

"Yes, sure, if it's genuine." I let the sarcasm show. "You've got plenty of nerve, but why would anyone believe a word you say?" Go on, Angelica, be indignant. When people get angry, they say things they shouldn't. But my little sortie against Angelica's credibility was wasted effort. Angelica didn't even flush. All she did do was sit quietly on my sofa and look beautiful and expensive. "Well?" I said.

"Can I look at the manuscript?" Beautiful, expensive, and single-minded.

"Wait a minute." Another idea was surfacing. "Before I say yes or no, who told you that I even *had* a manuscript?"

"I'm sorry," Angelica said, "I simply can't tell you that."

"In that case, the answer is no," I said. "Now, if you'll excuse me—"

"It was through one of your associates," Angelica said quickly.

"Which one?"

"There were rumors in London. Of course, there are always rumors." She smiled. She was doing a neat job of not answering. "But we learned that the manuscript was coming to this country. We made inquiries . . . and we traced the manuscript to you."

"Which one of my associates?" I asked again. This time, Angelica did look a little troubled.

"Please don't ask me that again, Alan," she said. "I won't tell you. But I will say that the person had no intention of betraying any secret." I sat back in my chair. All of this, whatever it meant, could be worked out later. Now, the question was what to do about Angelica.

"It's not convenient to let you look at the manuscript right now," I told her. She looked disappointed, but she nodded as if she'd been expecting a turndown. "But is there a phone where you can be reached?" I added.

"Of course!" She gave me the number.

"I'd like you to stay close to that telephone for the next few days. If I can arrange something, I'll call you."

"That would be fabulous." If she herself wasn't at the phone, Angelica assured me, somebody else would be. Day and night.

As I was ushering her to the door, she suddenly turned to face me. "Alan," she said softly, "I'm very sorry about what happened."

"Nothing happened," I said, thanking God it hadn't, "so there's nothing to be sorry about."

"You're sweet," said Angelica even more softly. She looked at me shyly through her long lashes. "Next time, maybe, things will be different."

"Could be," I said.

"Couldn't you give me just one quick peek before I go?" she asked appealingly, "I promise not even to touch." I pretended to consider.

"No," I said, "not today."

"Oh, well," she said, "I tried."

"And how!" I said. We both laughed. "Tell me one more thing," I said. "How much, I mean just roughly speaking, is a lot of money?"

"Well," she said slowly, "if this manuscript is what it's supposed to be. . . ."

"Go on," I said.

"Maybe a million to a million and a half dollars." I drew a deep, deep breath and let it out slowly.

"A million . . . and a *half*?"

"Something like that," Angelica said.

Good grief. Lucky Father Gilmary. Lucky Oratorians of Saint Loy. Then, an impish afterthought popped into my head. "Speaking of money . . ." I said.

"Yes?"

"Don't you owe me thirty dollars?" Angelica looked startled.

Then, her eyes narrowed ever so slightly, and she gave a little laugh.

"Absolutely not," she said. "The thirty dollars was for a guitar lesson and you never gave me a guitar lesson. So I don't see that I owe you anything."

"Fine by me," I said. "But I might just add it to the price." For some reason, my little wisecrack made her angry.

"All right, then," she muttered. She opened her handbag and fished out a gold pen and a leather-covered checkbook. "Here," she said, scribbling a check and handing it to me. "You really don't miss a trick, do you?"

"Have you any identification?" I asked her with a straight face.

"Any what?"

"You know . . . driver's license, credit cards, that sort of thing. You can't be too careful about accepting checks from strangers." Angelica gave me a dirty look. Then she decided that I was only being funny.

"You really are the most maddening person," she said. She snapped her handbag shut with a decisive click. "I don't understand why you won't even let me *see*—"

"Goodbye, Angelica," I said. "Stay by the phone."

"But of course," she said.

Back in the studio, I flopped down on the sofa to think. There was plenty to think about. For a start, I thought about the rather wide spread between Morlock's estimate of the worth of the manuscript and Angelica's. Morlock had mentioned six or seven thousand dollars. Angelica, to say the least, was in a different ballpark. I wondered about that, and I wondered whether or not Angelica Lederman, if that really was her name, actually did know anything about Renaissance manuscripts. It seemed unlikely, but everything about this situation seemed unlikely. I was still wondering when the intercom buzzer made its usual hoarse outcry.

This kind of playing also requires much cleverness and application, because you must know instantly how to take the various movements . . .

    Jean Rousseau, Treatise on the Viol
    (1687), p. 66

CHAPTER TEN

Empty teacups in hand, I hurried into the kitchen to cut off the croaking of the intercom. For once, when I mashed the earphone against my ear, an audible voice came out. Innocente. "Hey, Mister French, there's two guys gonna come up and see you." No names, naturally, just two guys. I mumbled something into the mouthpiece, which is clogged with at least six layers of greasy kitchen enamel, and hung the earphone back on its hook. As I did so, the doorbell rang loudly. Being a professional New Yorker, I peered through the peephole in the door before unlocking it. But that did me no good. Whoever was there was standing out of my line of vision. The next step was to hook the burglar chain in place. Then, I opened the door about two inches.

"Please, Mr. French," said a voice through the opening. I'd never heard the voice before. But I took note of the fact that it was a pleasant baritone and that it spoke in the accents of the well-educated Englishman. "Do let us in."

Well-educated Englishman or not, there's no point to being stupid. "Who are you and what do you want?" I said.

"You don't know us, Mr. French," said the voice, "but I assure you we're on a legitimate errand." There was a pause, during which I thought I could hear whispering. Then the voice said: "We're friends of Brother Martin's. And Father Gilmary's. From England."

Just to test them, I said, "I don't know any Father Gilmary."
There was a low chuckle from outside.

"Come now, Mr. French. We all know better than that. But
there's a good deal to talk about and we're busy men."

"What do we have to talk about?" I persisted. Another silence
and more whispering.

"Our watchword is, Good Queen Bess left the hell of a mess," a
second voice said cheerfully.

"All right," I said. "Go down to the lobby and I'll meet you
there. No, wait," I added quickly as my innate cowardice asserted
itself. "Across Amsterdam Avenue there's a pizza place, Nino's.
Go in and sit down at a table. I'll join you in five minutes. Get
yourselves some coffee."

"Mr. French. Really. . . ."

"See you at Nino's," I said firmly. "And by the way—"

"Yes, Mr. French?"

"I'll be watching from my window to make sure you both go
in."

They were both there when I walked in the door, huddling
uncomfortably at one of the tiny tables opposite the takeout
counter. Nino, whose real name is Nikos Nikeratos, was just
fetching them styrofoam cups of his unspeakable coffee. The two
men looked fairly English to me. One of them was big, with wide
shoulders and arms that bulged out the jacket of his wash-and-
wear suit. His ruddy face, blue eyes and straw-colored hair made
him a Central Casting version of Beatrix Potter's Farmer Mac-
Gregor. The other one was thin and dark-haired. He was wearing
a blue blazer with a crest on the pocket and a white shirt. I
couldn't tell whether his tie identified school, college, or club, or
whether his wife simply liked scarlet and gray striping.

Apart from us, the place was empty, which was a nice change
from its usual daytime state of being jammed with refugees from
the local junior high school.

"Well, gentlemen," I said. I shook my head to Nikos's offer of
coffee. Instead, I drew myself a lemon-and-lime fizzbang, with lots
of ice, from the soda machine on the counter. Then, I pulled up a

69

chair and sat down at the little table. "You wanted to talk. Go ahead and talk."

Farmer MacGregor gave me a reproachful look and cleared his throat. "There's no need to be so suspicious of us, sir. We're not here to cause you any problems. My name is Boddy, that's B-O-D-D-Y. The gentleman with me is Chief Inspector Cave. Dickie Cave, for short." Dickie Cave flashed me a thin-lipped, indifferent smile. "You'll have guessed, sir," Boddy went on, "that we're policemen."

"From England," I said sagely.

"That's right," said Cave, "England."

"You do have credentials, I suppose?" Silently, and in synchronization like a vaudeville act, they reached into their jackets. The cards in the dark blue leather cases they withdrew properly proclaimed Mssrs. Boddy and Cave to be members of Her Majesty's Metropolitan Police. "You're Scotland Yard!" I said. I was thrilled.

"No," said Cave, "Special Branch."

"Division of Art Fraud," said Boddy.

"Art Fraud?" A chill not attributable to the lemon-and-lime spread from my stomach outward.

"Yes, sir," said Boddy.

"Fake Leonardos," I said.

"That's right, sir," said Boddy, "and Picasso etchings signed by somebody or other. And Chagalls. You wouldn't believe how many Chagalls." He took a sip of his coffee and set the cup down carefully. "Extraordinary," he muttered.

"But of course, sir, this has nothing to do with you," Cave said.

"No, indeed," said Boddy.

"Well, then . . ." I said.

"We also look into situations where various categories of goods have been, er, illegally exported," Cave said smoothly. "Sometimes, chaps forget to declare things."

"It's the women, mostly," Boddy said morosely. "They come over, they buy whatever they fancy, spend thousands, then they think they can just wear their bits and pieces home from the shop. Silly, really."

70

"That's too bad," I said, "but I can't quite see—"

"The manuscript, Mr. French," Cave said. "We've come about the manuscript."

"What manuscript?" I asked. Neither man paid a bit of attention.

"Being an American, sir," Boddy said into the silence, "we thought you might not have known."

"Known what?"

"You need special permission to withdraw a national treasure from Great Britain, sir," said Boddy. "Or Ulster. That's Northern Ireland."

"I know where Ulster is," I said.

"Of course you do, sir," Cave said. "The manuscript known as 'Elizabeth's Boke,' or book, is considered a national treasure. Its removal from the country without a special export licence, even by its legal owner, is a crime."

"A felony," Boddy said with enjoyment. "You can go to prison for as long as three to five years. *And* you pay a fine."

"We have reason to believe that you are in a position to help us recover this manuscript," Cave said.

"I know of the manuscript," I said, "though I'd love to know how *you* know that."

"Information received," Boddy said.

"Mr. French, you have absolutely nothing to worry about, I assure you," Cave said soothingly. "We know you haven't *bought* the manuscript. We're quite certain you have nothing to do with its transport out of England. But you are . . . involved. You must see that it's in everyone's best interests, your own included, for the manuscript to be returned at once."

"Unlawful alienation of a national treasure is an extraditable offense," Boddy muttered as if to himself. "Doesn't matter whether you're the principal or only an accomplice."

"What exactly do you want from me?" I asked.

"Give the bloody thing back!" Boddy snapped, sudden venom in his voice.

"Now, now," said Cave. "The sergeant doesn't mean to be nasty, I'm sure. Do you, Sergeant Boddy? No. But still, sir, he's

71

quite right. You just turn the manuscript over to us. We'll give you a proper receipt for it. Then, we'll fly it back to England and hold it pending further inquiries as to its ownership."

"Ownership? You already know who owns it," I said, puzzled. "Father Gilmary, or rather his religious order. They're the owners."

"There seems to be some doubt on that score," Cave said slowly.

"Well, Father Gilmary claims—"

"We know what Father Gilmary claims." Cave was polite, but an edge of impatience sharpened his tone. "But that's nothing to do with you. Or me either, come to that. Our job, mine and Sergeant Boddy's, is simply to get hold of the manuscript and bring it home. The legal eagles can take it from there."

"You're making a mistake," I said. Cave's lips tightened skeptically, but he said nothing. "I haven't got the manuscript."

Cave and Boddy looked at each other.

"He hasn't got the manuscript," Boddy said.

"Dear, dear, how embarrassing," Cave said. "We've come to the wrong boyo."

"I don't," I said. "All I have is xeroxes."

"Copies?" Boddy asked. I nodded.

Cave picked up his styrofoam cup for the first time. He started to sample its contents, made a horrified face, and set the cup down. He said: "Look here, Mr. French. This isn't some odd kind of storybook game. We've traced that manuscript all the way from Wantage—that's near Oxford—to New York City. We want it back. We have strong reason to believe that you can help us get it back. We *think* you may not know the extent to which laws have been violated. Both English and American laws. We're willing to give you the benefit of the doubt."

"For a time," Boddy interjected.

"For a time," Cave echoed. "But you do have to cooperate. Perhaps you don't actually have the manuscript in your possession at this moment. Perhaps you do. I personally haven't the faintest. But we'll play along with you to this extent. In a week, you have that manuscript ready for us. One week."

"What if I can't?" I asked.

Cave looked at me wearily. "Well, Mr. French, we can't arrest you and hie you off to the Tower of London. But we can pay a visit to our good friend Larry Esposito. He's the Assistant U. S. District Attorney down on Federal Plaza. And we can swear out a felony warrant against you for conspiracy to commit grand larceny, larceny, accessory to grand larceny, receiving stolen goods, and failure to assist the police in the performance of their duties. Then our chums in the F.B.I. arrest you for us. You see?"

"I see," I said. "Thanks a lot."

Cave and Boddy didn't say anything. They just sat there, cop-fashion, as if they had all the time in the world.

Suddenly, I began to shake. I don't know whether it was because I was mad or because I was scared or simply because it had been one hell of an afternoon. But my hands were trembling, my pulse was racing, and I was having trouble with my breath control.

"Listen to me, you two bastards," I said between my teeth. "Listen *hard*." Cave went bolt upright in his chair with shock, and even Boddy looked startled. "The first move of *any* kind you make in my direction, and that includes my friends, and your precious manuscript goes up in smoke. I swear it. And I'll send the cinders right to the Prime Minister. Hell, I'll send them to the *Queen*!"

Cave's expression was almost comical. "You'd burn our treasure?"

"Try me," I said, the adrenalin singing in my veins.

"Well, God damn me black, Dickie," said Boddy. "Hello the mouse that roared." He shook with laughter, but his china-blue eyes wouldn't meet my own.

"I don't know what you think and I don't care," I said to Cave. "You leave us alone. We're in rehearsal and we're busy as hell," I added irrelevantly, "and you're not going to come near us."

"Then you admit you have the manuscript," Boddy said triumphantly.

"I admit bullfeathers," I said. "You started this. You can stop it. And you'd better."

This time, the silence dragged on for what seemed like hours. With one hand, Cave slowly revolved his cup of coffee, around

73

and around on its own ring of moisture. He looked up at me without expression. He opened his mouth to speak, shut it again, took out a cigarette and lit it. Finally he said: "There could conceivably be another alternative, Mr. French. Conceivably."

"What the hell are you talking about?" I said.

"Burn the manuscript and we could add one more charge, destruction of national property, to the list on that warrant." Cave looked around him. Nikos was busy in the back of the shop and well out of earshot, and we were still the only customers in the place. Even so, Cave lowered his voice. "But it might be possible for us to report to our superiors that the manuscript, while intact, was, er, no longer recoverable."

"There, now," said Boddy comfortably. "That's not a bad answer, is it?"

"Of course, we'd expect to recover something," Cave went on. "Some fraction of the value of the manuscript."

"In cash," said Boddy. "Dollars, for preference. But Deutschmarks or Swiss francs would be acceptable."

"You'd receive a certified copy of our report and the official approval," Cave said.

"And then?" I asked.

"That would be the end of it."

"I see," I said.

"You'll want to know what fraction of the value we'd expect to recover," Cave said easily. "Shall we say . . . whatever fraction that a hundred thousand dollars represents?"

Jesus Christ. I couldn't believe what was happening. Here were two British detectives, apparently perfectly genuine, who were soliciting a bribe from *me*. I wanted to say, like the girl in the dirty joke, "But I haven't even *met* you."

I got up from the table. My knees were unsteady. But for some odd reason I felt less frightened or angry than embarrassed, as if I'd committed some sort of social gaffe. "I'm leaving," I said. I tried to make my voice sound noncommittal. "I think I understand exactly what you have in mind. Naturally, I can't give you an answer on the spot."

"No, that's okay," said Boddy. "You go and have a natter with your principals."

"I will," I said, "and it may take a week or even ten days. Remember . . . I don't want to be followed, harassed, or wiretapped. If I even *think* you're playing games, I go into my firebug routine."

"That shouldn't be necessary," Cave said. He took a card out of his wallet, wrote a number on it and passed it to me. "When you're ready to talk. . . ."

"All right," I said. I stuffed the card into a pocket.

"Cheeribye," Boddy said pleasantly, like a stage Englishman. On my way out, I handed Nikos a couple of singles.

"If the gentlemen want another cup of coffee," I said, "be sure and take care of them." Nikos promised. I could conceive of no more dreadful revenge.

I was in no mood to go back to the apartment. Jackie and the others were due there at five-thirty for a rehearsal. I knew I should do some warmups and at least read over the music. But it was only four o'clock and after the vile atmosphere of Nino's the warm October sunlight felt good. Besides, if I went home, the phone might ring or the intercom might squawk. Or orcs might be lurking in the hallway by the elevator door, waiting to kidnap me and drag me off to the mines of Moria. If I took a walk, the orcs might get bored and go kidnap someone else.

So I turned south down Amsterdam Avenue to Seventy-ninth Street and wandered westward toward my favorite warm-weather loafing-spot, the Hudson River boat basin.

I kept glancing around furtively for orcs. But unless the bag lady drowsing amid her treasures on a bench in the park was an orc, nobody was taking any interest in me. I let myself in through the gate and went down the wooden steps onto the wharf. It was deserted. As always, it smelled of paint, tar, and the river. This year's sensation among the West Side boat people was an Indonesian prau. I sat down with my back against a piling, stared at the big carved sailboat as it swung at its moorings and listened to the

75

suck of the tidal current. I felt my body slowly relax. But my brain, needless to say, did not relax with it.

Obviously, the Antiqua Players was sailing into waters at least as murky as the Hudson off Seventy-ninth Street. And down in those waters, some outsize fish were circling slowly. Fish Number One was how on earth, or in the waters beneath the earth, all three of my afternoon companions, taking Boddy and Cave as one, had managed to conclude that Alan French was the man in charge of Elizabeth's Boke or book. Of course, the answer was as inescapable as the hydraulic metaphor that went with it. There had to be a leak somewhere in Father Gilmary's security arrangements. But where? And why was it leaking the wrong information? I was damned if I knew.

Far more disquieting, not to say scary, was this bid for a bribe. As apprehensive as I was, I managed to grin about one thing. Boddy and Cave had put an end forever to my romantic notions about British policemen. I was damned if I knew what to do about Boddy and Cave, either. The one thing I did know was that Father Gilmary had to be told about them, and told quickly.

Other, lesser thoughts also percolated in my mind. If I had climbed into bed with Angelica Lederman, would she have told me more about herself and her mysterious clients? I doubted it. Climbing into bed with Angelica would have been delicious, and I, or at least one part of me, was extremely sorry to have missed the experience. But Angelica, whatever she did let slip in bed, was not the sort to let slip any secrets. And Jackie Craine, if she ever found out that I'd been dallying with Angelica, was not the sort to accept as an excuse that I'd only been spying out enemy territory. She wouldn't believe that for a minute, and then I'd really be in trouble.

Suddenly, so suddenly it made me blink, it came to me that if Jackie were one good-looking girl and Angelica another, I probably would have tried my luck with Angelica. But Angelica had used music as an excuse to slip inside my guard, while Jackie wasn't just a good-looking girl but a real musician. For some reason too deep to analyze, this more than anything else had made me back away from temptation. I wasn't altogether happy about myself for reacting to Angelica as I'd done, but at least my crooked thoughts hadn't led me down a crooked path.

The sun was just burying itself in a mass of smog above the highrises on the New Jersey cliffs. I shivered a little. It was time to go. I stood up, stretched and walked back toward the gate. The sea-creatures, great and small, were still swimming about in my brain. But as I strolled, I did manage to make one decision. The right thing to do was to cash Angelica's check and take Jackie out for the best Chinese dinner thirty dollars would buy.

By the time I reached my building, it was nearly dark. Lights were going on in the windows along Amsterdam Avenue. I laughed at myself for being nervous on the streets, but it was cozy and comforting to ride the elevator up to my floor—Innocente wasn't around—and to hear through the apartment door the sound of Jackie's viol.

I put my key in the lock and opened the door with a cheerful greeting on my lips. But I never had a chance to utter it. As I stepped across the threshold, the phone began to ring. I waved hello to Jackie and picked it up. It was Father Gilmary.

"I was just going to call you," I began.

"Never mind about that," he said. His voice was thick with strain. "There's been trouble. I want you up here at once."

"What's wrong?"

"Brother Simon's been attacked. And the manuscript . . ."

"What about the manuscript?" I asked, dreading the reply.

"It's disappeared."

Many Drudge and take much Pains to Play their Lessons very Perfectly [but] They do not Labour to find out the Humour, Life, or Spirit of their Lessons . . .

Thomas Mace, Musick's Monument
(1676), p. 147

CHAPTER ELEVEN

The heater in the rented Plymouth conked out about forty miles up the Taconic Parkway. I was glad I'd made Jackie take along a warm coat. Despite the urgency in Father Gilmary's voice—and despite something else: was it fear?—we hadn't left right away. Instead, we'd taken enough time to have a cup of soup and a sandwich. And we'd waited for Ralph to show up for rehearsal, so someone would know what had happened and tell the others.

"I still can't believe it." I took my eyes off the road and gave Jackie a quick look. She sat huddled in her coat, only her face and one hand visible in the dim light from the dashboard.

"I can," I said. "After the day I've had, I'd believe anything."

"Tell me more about Angelica," Jackie said.

"There isn't that much to tell," I said. There was a silence. "There *is* that much to tell."

"I thought so. Was she . . . is she good-looking?"

"Mmmm. So-so."

"No, really. Tell me."

"Jackie, she's absolutely spectacular. There's only one thing wrong. With the way she looks, I mean."

"What?"

"She's not Jackie Craine."

78

"Alan, what are you trying to tell me?"

"I thought you'd never ask." As matter-of-factly as I could, I described exactly what had gone on—really, what hadn't gone on—in the bedroom that afternoon. When I finished, I stole another look at Jackie. She hadn't moved, except that her fingers were absently twisting and untwisting a strand of her dark hair. "Do you believe me?" I asked her.

"Yes, as a matter of fact, I do," she said.

"Well, that's something, anyway."

"For goodness' sake," she burst out, "what do you want me to do, say thank you, kind master Alan, for not sleeping with Angelica?"

"Hey," I said.

"Well, *do* you?"

"Do I what?"

"Want me to say thank you, I forgive you except that there's nothing to forgive, go through all of that bullshit?" When Jackie uses words like "bullshit," things are serious.

"Jackie . . ." I tried to keep my voice calm.

"What is it?"

". . . you're having your doubts about us, aren't you?"

"No. Yes. Oh, *Christus*, I don't know!" Almost exasperatedly, she began to cry.

Thank God, I had a clean handkerchief. "Here." She blew her nose once, twice and sniffled like a little girl. "But Jackie," I went on, "it's not really about Angelica Lederman, is it?"

"No," she said, "it's not."

"It's about music, isn't it?"

"How did you know?" she asked me wonderingly.

"I figured it out," I said, "and I even think I know what's worrying you."

"Tell me," Jackie said.

For a moment, I had to bend my efforts to getting the Plymouth around a fat station wagon that, like a politician in an election year, wanted to go very, very slowly down the middle of the road. Then I said: "I think you think you're better than I am. A lot

79

better. And I think you're scared of what that could do to us if we got married."

"You could be right," Jackie said. Then, slowly, "Am I better?"

I hesitated. But the thing I'd realized at the boat basin had to have its day. "You are," I said reluctantly. "Technically, you're much stronger. Musically, too. Just in the past few months."

"Oh, Alan," Jackie said.

It was my turn to burst out angrily. "What the hell are you going to do about it, cut off your fingers? You're better, that's all."

"And you don't like it," Jackie said.

"Of course I don't like it," I answered. "I don't like it for a lot of reasons, the first one being plain old-fashioned envy. The second . . ." I was silent, groping for the words to fit my scattered thoughts.

"The second?" Jackie prompted.

"I guess it's something like this. If you really are that much better than I am, and you are, then . . . won't I always be tempted to give up? To quit practicing. To say, let Jackie look after the music."

"If you did do that," Jackie said, "it would be awful. Is there anything we can do?" I breathed in a chestful of chilly, gasoline-scented air.

"I certainly hope so," I said. "Because apart from posing this monstrous threat to my ego, you happen to be the young damsel with whom I am passionately in love."

"Oh," Jackie said in a subdued voice.

"Yes, 'oh,'" I said. With some difficulty, I passed a laboring Fiat. The experience made me wonder how I was ever going to get the Plymouth up the hill to the monastery.

"You *are* good, you know," Jackie said. "Really."

"I am adequate technically," I recited, "and I have a strong musical feeling. That's what Mrs. Prodgers told my mother when I was in eighth grade. It was true then and it's still true now. I'm a journeyman fiddler and a journeyman flute-player. There are at least eighty violinists in the New York metropolitan area who can play my socks off. Ditto flautists. Am I right? Be honest." The unhappy silence from the passenger seat was all the corroboration

I needed. "That's okay," I went on after a moment. "Everybody can't be Heifetz. Or Rampal."

"Alan . . . stop the car."

"Stop the car? What for?"

"Because I want to kiss you."

That was different. I hit the indicator and the brake, swung off the pavement onto the grass, switched off the lights and the ignition and turned to Jackie. She wasn't wearing any perfume, subtle or otherwise. It took me a couple of seconds of exploration to realize that, under her coat and her sedate black sweater, she wasn't wearing anything else, either.

"You. Are. My. Own. True. Love," Jackie said, articulating the monosyllables with great care and kissing me with enthusiasm between each one. "And we are going to Solve Our Problem."

"Shut up," I said. My hands were not idle.

"We glug a wug this ow," Jackie murmured against my mouth. We both laughed.

"No doubt," I said, "but not right now."

"Why not?"

I kissed the tuft of hair that stuck up from her left eyebrow. "Because trying to get at you in this car is dislocating my spine," I said, "and because we really should be speeding to the scene of the crime."

"Okay," Jackie said doubtfully, "if you say so. But . . . will we be all right?"

"Sure we will," I said confidently. What else could I say? I breathed a silent prayer that we would indeed be all right. Then I let go of Jackie and started the car. "Of course, you have to promise to play very badly from now on."

"I promise," Jackie said. She giggled. "How badly?"

"We'll have to rehearse it," I said.

"I see." She smiled and reached over with her left hand to pat my right hand, at rest on the steering wheel. When our hands touched, I could feel the little pads of callus on her fingertips that had built up from pressing the strings of her gamba hour after hour, day after long day, for years.

"Sure we'll be okay," I said. "We belong to the same union."

81

She didn't answer, but I must have reassured her, because she sat back in her seat, yawned and stretched that fine body. Within a few miles, she was sound asleep.

By the time we reached the turnoff to the monastery, it was after ten o'clock. Once we'd left the parkway, the country darkness had settled around us. I'd seen nothing on the road except an occasional pickup truck, noticed nothing except the red and blue neon in the windows of the small roadside taverns. From the base of the monastery hill, no lights at all were visible. Only the hill itself bulked large and dark against the starry sky. I felt a sudden enormous reluctance to turn up the slope. It wasn't fear. It was my nerves signaling me that they'd had enough for one day. It would be so nice, they told me, simply to turn the car around and head for the nearest motel. No more Morlock, no more Boddy and Cave. Just Jackie, and then a good night's sleep.

From somewhere nearby, an owl hooted like the voice of doom. I jumped. "Jesus Christ!" That woke Jackie.

"What's wrong?" she asked.

"It's okay," I said. "We're nearly there." The Plymouth wasn't happy about it and neither was I, but up the hill we went. In second, all the way.

The light over the front door helped us while we fished our bags out of the back of the car and picked our way over the gravel to the entrance. The fact that the light was on was a bad sign. If Brother Simon had been operational, that light would have been off until he came to harass the caller.

As we neared the door, it opened. An anxious Brother Martin stood in the doorway. "It's you, is it, Mr. French?"

"It's me," I said ungrammatically, "and I've brought somebody with me. Miss Craine."

"Yes, yes, of course," Brother Martin muttered nervously. "Come in, both of you. Father is *very* anxious to see you."

"Good grief," I heard Jackie say under her breath as she caught her first sight of the long hallway and the massive staircase. "Wasn't there some crazy German prince—?"

"Mad King Ludwig of Bavaria," I said. "He was a good friend of Wagner's, remember?"

82

"Um-m. At least, I think so."

"This way." Brother Martin shepherded us agitatedly up the stairs and along the dimly lit corridor. "Such a dreadful thing," he kept on saying, "such a dreadful, dreadful thing." I noticed that he never let himself look directly at Jackie. His gaze kept sliding toward her, then away, as though she were a temptress sent to jar him loose from his vows. "In here," he said, indicating the library.

Father Gilmary was standing by the big worktable. His handsome face was lined with fatigue and strain. "Hullo, French," he said shortly, "good of you to come on such brief notice." He gave Jackie the ghost of a smile. "And you must be—"

"Miss Craine," I said, "Jackie Craine."

"Oh, yes," Father Gilmary said. "Well, Miss Craine, it's a pity we have to meet under such unfortunate circumstances." He shrugged wearily. "I don't suppose there's very much you can do, either of you. It's gone, that's all." I started to ask him what had happened, but he went on as if I hadn't spoken. "What I would like to know," he said with sudden intensity, "is how they knew we had it in the first place." As he uttered the words, he fastened his eyes on me. "I'd like to know that."

Jackie was quicker than I was. "Oh, no!" she exclaimed. "If you think Alan . . . if you think any of us had anything to do with this, you're absolutely, totally wrong! That's crazy!"

Father Gilmary gave her another faint smile. "I'm sure Mr. French is grateful for the testimonial, my dear. I know I would be. But all the same, one can't help wondering, can one?" He gestured toward the worktable. On it was the heavy steel box I remembered from my earlier visits. Its lid was thrown back and the box gaped disconsolately open.

"What in God's name happened!" I asked thoughtlessly.

"Ah." From deep in Father Gilmary's throat came a mirthless chuckle, or perhaps a sob. "In God's name, indeed." He was irritated with me but too well-trained to show it. Then he sighed. "I've been over all of that with the police. But I suppose it can't hurt to go over it again. That is—" once again, his voice grew sharp with suspicion "—if you don't already know the story."

83

"Forget that," I said. "Apart from everything else, if I have to, I can prove where I was for nearly every minute of the day."

"I'm sure you can, my dear chap," Father Gilmary said. "Of course you can. Please forgive me. It's just that I'm so tired. . . . ."

"We understand," Jackie said.

"Why don't we all sit down?" Father Gilmary led us to the far end of the library, where a sofa and chairs were grouped around a huge, cold fireplace. "Martin, do you think you could do us some tea? I'm sure our guests would like some. The kettle's on downstairs."

"Yes, Father, of course."

"And make sure you have some yourself."

"Yes, Father."

"Now . . . ." Father Gilmary said when Brother Martin had left. "Where shall I begin?" His story was quickly told and seemed perfectly straightforward. About eight that morning, the Oratorians' hosts, the Recollects of St. Anthony, had all piled into a yellow school bus and had gone off to a day-long outing somewhere in the Hudson Valley. They had left Brother Simon behind, as they always did, to look after the monastery. A little before noon, Father Gilmary and Brother Martin had taken the Recollects' Volkswagen into Leicester, the nearby town, to do some shopping— "you know, razor blades, that sort of thing." They'd stayed in Leicester for lunch at the local inn. I gathered that Brother Simon's Saturday special, fried-egg sandwiches on day-old bread, had had something to do with that decision.

After lunch, they'd driven straight back to the monastery. They'd noticed nothing peculiar on the way. But when they reached the front entrance, there was Brother Simon, face-down on the flagstones. "Somebody had fetched him an almighty wallop," said Brother Martin, munching, as he dispensed the tea and passed around a plate of chocolate-covered graham crackers.

Leaving Brother Martin to watch over Brother Simon, who was semiconscious and bleeding profusely, Father Gilmary rushed inside to call an ambulance and to check on his treasure. "As soon as I rang off, I ran to the library. The box was on the little table

84

where it was always kept. It was closed but not locked. When I opened it up, the manuscript was gone." Immediately, Father Gilmary called the police. Within minutes, the ambulance arrived. The crew loaded Brother Simon aboard and departed for the hospital, twelve miles away. "I wanted to send Martin with poor Simon," Father Gilmary said, "but I thought the police would want to speak with him, so I kept him with me."

About a half-hour later, the police appeared, in the person of a young state patrolman. "When I began to tell him about the manuscript, he stopped me and radioed for help." After that, things apparently got out of hand. Soon, there were three or four State Police cruisers at the monastery, all with their doors open and their radios blaring as the patrolmen tramped around the main house and the outbuildings and questioned Father Gilmary and Brother Martin again and again about what had taken place. "They seemed more interested in our accents than they were in the robbery," Father Gilmary said wryly. I nodded. It was easy to imagine what up-country state policemen would make of an assault-and-burglary case featuring two English priests and a missing Elizabethan manuscript.

In the midst of all of this, up the hill came the yellow school coach laden with the Recollects of St. Anthony. "They had to be put in the picture, you understand, and then the police began asking *them* all sorts of questions."

At length, an unmarked police car delivered State Police Lieutenant Reginald A. Catapana to the scene. Lieutenant Catapana sent away the uniformed troopers and took charge of the case himself. The Lieutenant's theory, expressed after five minutes of investigation, was simple. Somebody, "probably a local kid," drove up to the monastery and rang the front doorbell. When Brother Simon answered, the Perpetrator hit him over the head and made his way into the building in search of booty. He found the steel box in the library. Assuming naturally that a locked strongbox held something of value, the Perpetrator picked the lock and drove off with the manuscript.

Father Gilmary eyed me quizzically. He made a small noise in his throat. "Perhaps I'm mistaken about your American police methods," he said, "so I'll make no comment."

After a while, Lieutenant Catapana told Father Gilmary that he wanted "to do some checking" in Leicester. As soon as Catapana drove off, Father Gilmary called the hospital. They told him that Brother Simon was in "stable condition." The phrase puzzled him. "We're used to something more definite," he explained. So he, Brother Martin and Father Antoninus O'Rourke, the superior of the Recollects, all drove into Northborough to the hospital.

"We tiptoed into the room and saw Simon lying there, poor man," said Brother Martin, "and he was trying to *talk* to us."

"He was certainly muttering something," Father Gilmary corrected him, "but whether he was talking to us, that would be hard to say."

"What *was* he saying?" asked Jackie.

"Well, you know, that was the strange part," Brother Martin said. "Simon once told me that he'd never read the Old Testament. Couldn't stand it, he said, all that doom and gloom. Yet here he was, going on about Ezekiel."

"Ezekiel?" I asked.

"Over and over again, that's what he was saying. 'Ezekiel, go to Ezekiel.'" Father Gilmary shook his head. "I'm afraid the old boy must have been wandering."

They waited by the bedside for a few minutes, hoping that Brother Simon would wake up. But he remained semiconscious, and before long a head nurse chased them out of the room. They came back to the monastery and ate their supper. Then, after what Brother Martin called "a bit of a pray" for Brother Simon, they called me.

"I hope you're quite clear in your mind about me," I said, "because I've done quite a bit of suffering for the cause myself today."

"What on earth do you mean?" Father Gilmary asked. Quickly, I told them about my lunch with Tarleton Morlock and an edited version of the rest of my afternoon. Angelica Lederman's name meant nothing to Father Gilmary. But then I described what had happened with Boddy and Cave, and watched his attentiveness give way to anger. "That's outrageous!" he said more than once.

But by the time I had finished, he was calm again. "Look here," he said, "I want you to know the absolute truth about this. Our solicitors have gone into the matter exhaustively. The Crown has no rights whatever in our manuscript. And it has never been declared a national treasure, so it can leave England quite legally. I'm dreadfully sorry these people approached you. I can't think how . . ." His voice trailed off, and he winced as if a sudden nasty thought had struck him. "Good Lord!" he exclaimed suddenly, and then fell silent again. A moment later, he said unhappily: "You know, I blame myself very much for this. I'm afraid I'm the one who led those chaps to you."

The thing was simple. He and Father Antoninus O'Rourke of the Recollects had been in the local drugstore buying something prosaic, like toothpaste or razor blades. This was a day or two after we'd signed our contract together. "Antoninus asked me about our progress," Father Gilmary said, "and I remember saying, 'It's all in the hands of Alan French and his friends,' or something like that." And he'd been overheard. "Is your Sergeant Boddy a biggish man with a red face and blue eyes?"

I nodded.

"That's it, then," Father Gilmary said. He stood up and moved restlessly around the room, deep in thought. "You leave this to me," he said finally. "I won't have this sort of thing. It's not going to be easy to stop, but I'm going to try. You had no witnesses, I suppose? No, no, of course not, these are experienced men. An ugly business they're doing, though. Well, let me do a bit of phoning and cabling. Perhaps we can give our friends a bit of a comeuppance."

"I'd love that," I said. Privately, I couldn't imagine what sort of comeuppance a Roman Catholic priest could give a couple of senior British cops. But what was the use of worrying Father Gilmary with that thought? He had enough to worry about. In fact, he looked the way I felt. I was relieved when he suggested that we pack it in for the night.

"There's nothing more we can do about the manuscript," he said in an empty voice. "We do have to think what the next step should be, about your concert and all of that. But we'd best sleep on it. We can discuss it in the morning. Martin, has Father Antoninus got things ready for our guests?"

"Absolutely, Father," said Brother Martin. "He's even lighted a fire in the one cell and aired the beds."

"I'll say good night, then," said Father Gilmary, rising, "and God bless you both. Brother will show you to your rooms."

"It's only just a short way," said Brother Martin, leading us down what seemed in the gloom like a series of endless corridors. "We've put your bags right in your rooms. No, no trouble at all." He gazed back at us anxiously. "I hope you won't mind separate rooms. Father Antoninus insists, you see. And anyway, I can unlock the connecting door. Here we are!" He pushed open two massive doors and switched on lights in each room.

"Cells" really was a misnomer for largish rooms with high ceilings, cream-colored plaster walls, big windows and dark red carpeting on their varnished oak floors. A small fire crackling in the iron fireplace of the near room did its best to take the chill out of the air. True, there was an extraordinarily ugly prie-dieu in one corner and an alarming *Martyrdom of Saint Sebastian* on the wall opposite the door. The far room had no fireplace, but it did have a portrait of Saint Francis feeding his birds. The narrow beds with their green chenille spreads looked less than inviting. But all in all things could have been much worse.

Brother Martin bustled awkwardly about the room like a bellhop, opening and shutting drawers and plumping up pillows. Then, with a conspiratorial wink, he used a large key to unlock the door between the two rooms. He was still not quite meeting Jackie's eye. "Bathroom just across the hall," he announced finally. We thanked him and he made his exit, dragging shut behind him the heavy hall door of the room with the fireplace. In the silence, Jackie and I exchanged glances, relieved to be alone. Alone, that is, except for Saint Sebastian.

"Holy Christmas, what a day!" I fumbled with the knot in my tie, my fingers suddenly wooden with fatigue.

"You poor thing," Jackie said as I hoped she would. "Stand still and let me help you." She came over to me and stood very close to work on my tie. She smiled up at me, her eyes bright. I found myself growing rapidly less tired.

"Aren't you nice?" I purred lecherously.

"I *am* nice, now that you mention it," Jackie said. "There. Now, don't just stuff the tie in your pocket the way you usually do. Hang it neatly over the back of the chair." By mutual consent, we were making our headquarters the room with the fire. Jackie brought in her small overnight case from the other room, unpacked it and began to get undressed.

"Where's your sexy black nightgown?" I demanded.

"Shh-h! He'll hear us." We both looked over at Saint Sebastian and laughed. No doubt about it, having that many arrows shot into you is daunting, not only for you but for onlookers as well. "You keep an eye on him and an ear open for Father Antoninus," Jackie said. "I'll go brush my teeth." She finished undressing, wrapped a worn old flannel bathrobe around her and walked barefoot across the hall. I added a couple of sticks to the fire and poked at it cautiously, with little result. Then it was my turn to step across the hall. When I got back, Jackie was sitting gingerly on the edge of the bed. "Alan?"

"Hmmm?"

"It's cold." Fire or no fire, it *was* cold. "Did you bring any pajamas?"

"Never a one," I said.

"I didn't, either."

"Well, let's get it over with," I said, peeling back the bedspread.

"You first," said Jackie. I kicked off the sheepskin-lined slippers she'd given me for my last birthday and slid into the bed.

"Aggh!" I moaned like Charlie Brown. The sheets were clammy newsprint. Long ago, the single blanket had been chosen for its thinness by someone utterly dedicated to the mortification of the flesh. I clenched my teeth tightly to keep them from chattering and forced a grin. "Come on," I said, "It's not too bad now. I'm getting it nice and warm."

Doubtfully, Jackie switched off the light, shed her robe, and crawled in beside me. For one split second, there was breathless silence. Then, "You LIAR!" she yelled, wriggling frantically in an effort to keep her circulation going. "I'll fix YOU!" She grabbed the sheet and the blanket and in a series of lightning twists wound them tightly around herself, leaving me bare and shivering. "Hah!" From her cocoon, she gave me a triumphant glare.

"No way!" I said to her. The first thing I did was to wriggle out from between Jackie and the icy wall. Then I bounded across the floor to the other room flung back the bedspread there and tore loose the blanket, which I wrapped around me. "Now, young lady!" I said, coming through the door.

"No . . . !" Jackie squeaked, but I was remorseless. I unpeeled the nest in which she was curled, threw the second blanket over it and her and wedged myself in with her. "Ooooh! Your feet are like ice!"

"It's all your fault," I said. I got both arms around her and squeezed. All those good warm parts of Jackie pressed up against me. After a minute or so, my heart stopped pounding from cold and began pounding for other reasons.

"You, sir, are an unfeeling wretch," Jackie said in her best Lady Booby manner. But when I kissed her, she kissed me back energetically. Her bare arms slipped around me, and she gave a happy sigh.

"Unfeeling?" I mumbled into the softness of her breast.

"Well, that is the wrong word, I must admit," she said, and we laughed softly together in the dimness of the fading fire. What we began to do after that was no laughing matter.

Suddenly and infuriatingly, Jackie stiffened.

"What's wrong?" I asked.

"Shhh! Listen!" she whispered.

Someone was tapping, very softly, at our door.

"Oh, Christ," I said, "go away!" The tapping continued. Cursing, I disentangled myself from Jackie and the bedclothes and stood up. I slipped on pants, shirt and sweater and stuck my feet back in my slippers. Then I went over to the door. "Who's there?"

"Please," breathed a voice. Brother Martin's. "Let me in."

"For God's sweet sake," I began. Behind me, Jackie was out of bed, moving around, putting on her clothes.

"Please . . . I must talk to you."

"I'm decent," Jackie said a few seconds later. "Let the poor man in."

"Oh, thank you, thank you," said Brother Martin when I opened the door. "This is terrible, I know. But I must tell *someone.*"

He was weirdly dressed for a late-night conversation. At least, not too many of my friends would wear a priest's black shirt over green-and-orange striped pajamas, top off this ensemble with a plaid lumberjacket, and then go tiptoeing through the halls in shiny black rubber boots. But beneath his scraggling beard, Brother Martin's mouth was trembling and his fists were tightly clenched by his sides. So I bit back my laughter and waited.

"You'll think I'm an incredible fool," he said.

"Why, what have you done?" Jackie asked him gently.

"I *am* one," he said. He sat down on a bed, so hard that it creaked under his weight. All of a sudden, he bent over, hid his face in his hands and started to sob. His nails, I noticed, were bitten to the quick. "I *am* a fool," he said to the floor.

Jackie went over to him and put her arm around him. "Tell me," she said.

"Oh, God," Brother Martin said, sniffling. He wiped his nose with the back of his hand, as unself-conscious in his misery as a child. "I'm the one who did it."

"Did what?" I asked. "Hit Brother Simon?"

"Oh, no," he said, "not that. Worse. In a way. I'm the one who told about the manuscript."

"Who did you tell?" He sniffled again and blew his nose on the tissue Jackie pressed into his hand.

"It was in London," he said. "Before Father and I came over to the States. He sent me up to London to sort out some bits of business, pick up tickets, that kind of thing. It didn't take long, and I had some time before the train to Oxford," he explained pathetically.

91

"What happened?" This time, Jackie asked the question.

"I stopped in the Lyons's at Piccadilly for a cup of tea. I shouldn't have . . . Father says I should always come straight home. But I love Lyons's and I was hot and thirsty. I only had tea," he added half-defiantly. "No cakes or buns. And then she came."

"She?"

"She asked if she could share the table. She said she hated to ask most people, she never knew what they might do, but she hated to have her tea alone. She was so beautiful. . . ." His voice trailed off into silence, but then he said loudly: "If I were going to sin, you know, they would be carnal sins."

As a veteran carnal sinner myself, I was too embarrassed to say anything. But Jackie nodded understandingly and patted his shoulder.

Brother Martin looked directly at her for once and gave her a grateful smile. "We got talking," he went on. "She asked me the name of my community and I told her and she knew of us. That's unusual, you see. Then she said she'd done some work in university on religious communities after Henry the Eighth. That's unusual, too. But I'll tell you the truth," he said, staring down at his hands. "She could have said whatever she liked. I just wanted her to stay there, you know. . . ."

"And keep on talking," said Jackie.

"That's right," said Brother Martin.

"Then what happened?" I asked.

"Well, now, this was it. She said she often wondered whether any of those old communities had managed to save any of the good things they must have had. Pictures, old prayer books, that sort of thing. And I . . ." he grimaced at the memory, ". . . I told her. About the manuscript we'd had since the seventeenth century that came from the queen and how we'd smuggled it out of the palace and got it right out of England to Douai and held on to it. She asked me if we still had it. I said we did." He stopped, squeezing the knuckles of one hand hard with the fingers of the other. "She wore tiny little gold scallop-shells in her ears." He closed his eyes, as if to escape from the thought. Or else lose himself in it.

"Was she English?" I asked.

He thought about it, frowning. "No, now you mention it, I don't think she was. Why?" Then he burst forth passionately: "What difference could it possibly make? She was the most perfect woman I've ever seen and I let her trick me. . . ."

"Have you told Father Gilmary about her?" Jackie asked him.

To my horror, he started to sob all over again. "No. No, I couldn't. I should have told him, I know, but he would be so upset. So . . . disappointed." After a moment, he took hold of himself. He lifted his head and looked damply at us. His lips parted in a weak smile. "So now I've come to you instead. To confess myself. What a creature I am!" He said it with a kind of exhausted objectivity. I thanked God devoutly that I was no Brother Martin.

"Well, for what it's worth," I said, "I don't think you've done too much damage."

"Do you really mean that?" he asked me, his face suddenly hopeful.

"This girl," I told him. "Obviously, she had a pretty good idea of who you were and what you were before she arranged to sit down at your table."

"Yes, of course," he said. "I've thought of that. But still. . . ."

"Relax," I said. "You might have told her something, but I suspect you told her very little that she didn't already know." I didn't add that if the girl was who I thought she was, to wit, Angelica Lederman, he was lucky he hadn't agreed to go and steal the manuscript and *give* it to her. "Do me one favor, though."

"Yes, absolutely." His relief made him jittery. He jumped up from the bed and paced back and forth across the carpet.

"In the morning, tell Father Gilmary something about this girl. Say you met her on the train. . . ."

"Oh, no," he said seriously. "I couldn't lie to Father."

"All right, then," I said, "tell him the truth. You'll feel better.

But say that she already knew about the book. Because I think she already did."

"I will," Brother Martin said. "I'll tell him."

"One more thing," I said.

He looked at me with pathetic gratitude. "What is it?" he asked.

"If you ever see her again, be careful."

"Oh, I will. I will," he repeated with a strained smile. "Now, I *must* go. It's been wretched of me to impose myself like this. But you've been wonderful. I'll sleep tonight for the first time since . . . it happened." Jackie and I made suitable noises. At last, we got Brother Martin out the door.

What he did thereafter, I have no idea. But Jackie and I got undressed all over again, climbed into bed, exchanged one brief, chaste kiss and instantly went to sleep.

The Acciaccatura *is a Composition of such Chords as are dissonant with respect to the fundamental Laws of Harmony; and yet . . . produce that very Effect which it might be expected they would destroy.*
Francesco Geminiani, Rules for Playing
in a True Taste, &c. (1739)

CHAPTER TWELVE

I dreamed I was playing the Fifth Brandenburg Concerto. That's the one in D major where Bach pits the flute, violin, and harpsichord against the strings. For some reason—I think the other soloists were late for the concert—they had me doing all three main parts. The harpsichord sounded wonderful, which was quite a relief because I was sight-reading the music and also because I don't know how to play the harpsichord. The flute was under control, too. I was fingering it with my toes and bending over from time to time to blow into it. This was okay because it would go four or five bars at a time on one breath. But as usual I hadn't been practicing enough and my toes were getting tired and in three more bars I was going to have to bring in the violin. . . .

I woke up. The air in the room was Arctic, and so were my toes. The blanket had come unmoored in the night, and my feet were sticking out of the bottom of the bed. I tucked them back in. By my side, curled into a warm mound, Jackie slept peacefully on. It's remarkable what hard work, dedication, and a clear conscience will do for your ability to sleep. As for me, I'd been so busy in my dream that it was restful to lie awake. I thought vague thoughts about the missing manuscript, about Brother Martin and the beautiful girl I was sure was Angelica Lederman, about what was going to happen next. The strange thing was, I wasn't worrying about the manuscript. It would turn up or it wouldn't, but the music itself was safely copied and could never be lost or destroyed. I sighed, wriggled deeper under the inadequate covers and began to go over in my mind some of the problems we'd have to work out in rehearsal.

Wham-bam, wham-bam, dong! The noise of the handbell clanging outside in the corridor was appalling. For one nightmare moment, I wondered if the monastery was on fire. But then the clanging stopped, and in the sudden silence I could hear doors banging somewhere and footsteps scuffling slowly along. I glanced at my watch. Six-thirty. You are in a religious establishment, I reminded myself, and that hellish bell must have resounded to get the monks up from their pallets, or whatever it was they slept on, and on about their daily round. At this hour, they were probably at prayer, but at all events they were up, and so, I decided, was I.

I sat up in bed, then got up. Before braving the journey to the bathroom, I tossed a couple of pieces of kindling on the smouldering remnants of the fire, more as a gesture than because I expected any result. But when I came back from shaving and brushing my teeth, the fire was crackling away bravely and the room, if not warm, was at least capable of sustaining human life.

Jackie, half-awake, rolled over in bed and pulled the blankets all the way up over her head.

"It's no use," I told her. "Day has dawned, and you with it."

"Christus," she said, stretching. "Did somebody ring a horrible bell?"

"Somebody did," I said, "and since that moment there has been no peace."

"Throw me my bathrobe, Alan. Please?"

"Well, now," I said, "that depends."

"Please?" Jackie's small mouth tightened dangerously. "It's cold and we didn't get enough sleep last night and I'm tired, but I'm still being extremely polite and saying please. Okay?"

"Here," I said, handing her the bathrobe. "But I'm only doing it because I'm a coward, and if I don't not only will you not kiss me, which I want you to do, but you'll do something terrible to me when I'm not looking, probably when I'm sound asleep."

"That's because I'm a coward, too." But she did administer a small early-morning kiss.

A few minutes later, washed and dressed, we went hand in hand along the dim passageways of the house in search of breakfast. We never really did figure out the layout of the place. It seemed to consist largely of long corridors with limed-oak paneling and pictures of stags on the walls and cocoa-mat runners on the floors, like the illustrations of huge old resort hotels in coffee-table books about the vanishing American scene. But eventually we came to a staircase, walked down one flight, turned left and found ourselves amid a cluster of the Recollects of St. Anthony.

"Good morning," said one of the Recollects pleasantly. Despite the chill, he had on above his green khaki work pants only a cotton T-shirt. It portrayed a family of about eight rabbits. "God Bless This Mess," the T-shirt said. The only other odd thing about the Recollect was that he had almost no eyebrows.

Jackie and I hastily dropped each other's hands.

"Good morning," we said back.

"You'll want a bite of breakfast," said the Recollect. "Fine, fine. Just come along with us."

In a room beyond a fine set of glass doors, four or five vinyl-topped tables were set up for meals. More Recollects were grouped around the tables, but there were still plenty of empty seats. One long table held stacks of plates and wire racks of mugs and heavy glasses. At the far end, a young Recollect in a stained apron presided over a steaming pot of brownish cereal and a selection of other foods. Service was cafeteria-style, so we took our places in line.

"Oh, boy!" said somebody ahead of us. "Sweet rolls! Brother must have bought out the day-old store!" Sure enough, spread open on the table were cardboard bakery boxes of sticky pastry. The stuff did have a slightly battered, day-old look, but the Recollects were as thrilled as a bunch of schoolboys. With a hungry grin, one greyheaded monk scooped three of the things onto his plate. Watching him taught me more about the vow of poverty than a dozen theology textbooks could have done. The rest of breakfast was just as instructive. I settled for a tiny paper cup of

97

orange drink, two slices of Bunny Bread toast, and a china mug of pale, pale brown coffee. Jackie took one look at the offerings and poured herself a mug of tea.

"That's all you're having?" I asked her.

"That's all I want," she said.

"I hope you'll join us," said Bless-This-Mess as we made our way past the food table. "In fact, I insist." He led us to a table on the far side of the room and introduced us to Fathers John and Dan and Brothers Eric and Kenneth. Everybody nodded and bowed politely and went on eating sticky buns. We sat down, feeling decidedly out of place. Musicians learn to eat whenever and wherever they can, but the refectory of a monastery at seven-fifteen in the morning was stretching things. I wasn't at all sorry to see Brother Martin edging his way gently toward us. To my relief, he was looking far less agitated than he'd looked the night before.

"Please don't let me rush you," he said. "But as soon as you've finished, could you come have a word with Father?" His message delivered, Brother Martin sat down and in his turn devoured a plateful of sticky buns. I took a sip of coffee. It made me wish vindictively that Boddy and Cave were here. Not even Nikos the Greek pizza-maker could have concocted a more dreadful potion than this one.

Brother Martin extracted a paper napkin from the plastic holder in the center of the table and used it to wipe away a few remnants of sugar icing. "Are we ready?" he asked brightly. We were.

Once again, Father Gilmary was waiting for us in the library. He, too, was calmer than he'd been when we had seen him last. He ran a hand wearily over his forehead. "First of all," he said, "I feel I owe you an apology. And you, too, my dear." He gave Jackie a faint smile. "Yesterday, before you arrived and even afterward, I couldn't for the life of me see how anyone could have known or even guessed at the manuscript's existence. Unless . . . unless there had been an indiscretion on your part.

"But now, of course, I realize that some information could have got out through, er, other channels." He glanced over at Brother Martin, who went crimson with embarrassment. "However it happened, it's water under the bridge. But I did want to say that my

98

suspicions were wrong and unworthy and I am sorry for having given way to them."

"I'm glad you feel that way, Father," I said. "It makes things a lot easier for us."

"Good," said Father Gilmary. "Now, that brings me to the next point, the music. I take it your rehearsals are going well?"

"Well enough," I said. Actually, they hadn't even begun. I was still transcribing and arranging the music from the manuscript. What we were playing in rehearsal was the material for the three other concerts we had booked for October and November. But it would be less than tactful to try to explain to Father Gilmary that we really didn't need two months of rehearsal time on his music, that two good solid weeks would be more like it. So I simply said: "We were planning to invite you down to listen when we had something worth hearing."

"Why, that's very kind of you." Father Gilmary looked momentarily less troubled. Then he said, "At first, after what happened yesterday, I thought perhaps we should simply cancel. After all, the purpose of the concert is to publicize the book, and if we don't have the book. . . ."

"You can't see the need for the concert," I said.

"Exactly."

"But that would be a shame," Jackie said.

"Not to mention the loss of the deposit for the hall," I added.

"Well, I thought so, too," said Father Gilmary. "And I think we had better go on with the plans for the concert regardless of the, er, fate of the manuscript. Besides, I suppose there always is the possibility that the manuscript will turn up."

"Could I ask you something?" I said.

"Certainly you may," said Father Gilmary.

"Why is this so terribly important to you? I mean, I can understand that your, um, organization wants the money from a sale."

"It's not just a matter of *wanting*, Mr. French. It's a matter of need. Our community has a purpose, you understand, beyond mere survival."

"Yes, indeed," Brother Martin broke in loudly. "To glorify the sacred name of Our Savior and Lord Jesus Christ. Through work and prayer."

"Quite." Father Gilmary frowned slightly, as if he found Brother Martin's fervor a bit unprofessional. "It is an obligation upon us under our Rule to expend the resources of the community, at need, for this purpose and no other. Today, we are in need." He got to his feet and paced a few steps, first away from us, then back. "I myself, speaking personally, should like nothing better than *not* to have to sell the Queen's Book. It's a beautiful thing. But . . . we have nothing else left to sell. I really have no choice. *Had* no choice, I should say."

"I understand," I said. "Well, the money from the concert will add up to something. We might even get a record contract out of it. And as you say, maybe the book will turn up."

Father Gilmary shrugged and smiled. "I'm praying for all of these things. And for Brother Simon's recovery." Guiltily, I realized that I'd forgotten all about Brother Simon. "I called the hospital at six o'clock," Father Gilmary went on, "and they said he was asleep and doing as well as could be expected."

"Had he said anything at all?" Jackie asked.

"Apparently not. But if he does, I'll let you know immediately, of course." Father Gilmary sat down again. I felt the time had come to get going, and I said as much.

"Yes, yes," Father Gilmary said, "absolutely. There's no point to your staying here. You go back to New York and . . . get on with it. But we're most grateful for your coming up. It has certainly cleared the air." He turned to Jackie and said, "Miss Craine, I'm happy to have met you. Last night, I admired your spirited defense of Mr. French. The next time we meet, the circumstances will undoubtedly be better."

"I certainly hope so," Jackie said, and on that note we parted with our patron. Twenty minutes later, I was edging the car back down the hill toward New York.

[Singing-men are to be] men of worship . . . shew-ing in descant clene voysed, well released and pro-nouncying, eloquen in reding; sufficiaunt in organes playing, and modestiall in other other maner of behaving . . .

Liber Niger (c. 1472), Ordinance 50.

CHAPTER THIRTEEN

As soon as we dumped the rental clunker and let ourselves into my apartment, Jackie began scrambling eggs and I sat down at the telephone. I reached Ralph and Terry without trouble and filled them in on our adventures of the past thirty-six hours, urban and rural. David, as usual, was another story.

"Jackie, is David still at Judy's?" Judy was the girl after Rhoda from Woodmere. Or maybe the girl *after* the girl after Rhoda from Woodmere. I wasn't quite sure, and it didn't really matter. All of David's girls tend to be large and dark-haired and managerial.

"Wait a minute," Jackie called back from the kitchen. She was probably flipping through her address book, which she somehow keeps perfectly legible and perfectly up to date. My address book is the cardboard back of a pad of music paper, taped on the wall next to the kitchen phone. It is not legible. It is not up to date. "Try him at Jake's," Jackie said. "I've got a note that says he can be reached at Jake's until October twenty-third."

"Okay, I remember." Jake is the *luthier*, the violin-maker and stringed instrument repairer, who finances David between jobs and girls. He always accepts David's lute as collateral for a loan. When the loan money is gone, he gives David repair work to do in ex-change for nominal pay and a place to sleep in back of the shop. David loves this arrangement. Jake's shop smells so vilely of the

101

hides Jake boils up to make his glues that none of David's girl friends can stand to go near the place. "How else could I be alone to practice?" David asks deadpan.

The phone at Jake's rang the usual fourteen or fifteen times. Finally, Jake answered. I asked for David. "Who wants him?" Jake asked suspiciously. When I told him, he grunted, dropped the receiver on the workbench and went away, possibly forever. I held on grimly. Jake and Brother Simon, two of a kind.

David eventually picked up the phone. When I told him what had been happening, he gave a low whistle. "This is getting pretty heavy," he said. "Maybe we should just give the old geek back his music, huh?"

This could mean only one thing. David had gone into hiding from Judy and didn't want to leave the shop for rehearsals. A familiar syndrome. "Sure," I said, "and what about getting our four thousand dollars back?"

"Oh, yeah," David said. "That could be a problem, right?"

"Right," I said. In fact, I hadn't the slightest doubt that we could get out of our contract with Father Gilmary and get back at least some of the four thousand dollars. But it was a fact of David's life that once you turned over money to somebody else, even your mother, you weren't ever going to see it again.

He thought it over. "I guess we better keep on going, then," he said.

"I guess so," I said. "Besides, we have to rehearse for those other concerts."

"True. You got any money?"

"I can get your lute out of hock," I said, "if that's what you mean."

"I really need a place to stay," David said.

"I bet you do," I said, thinking of Judy. Judy was very intense.

"Huh?"

"Nothing. You want to stay here for a while?"

"Hey, could I? Just for a few days?" I was definitely right. Judy was hot on his trail.

"Good," I said. "Get your stuff together and take a cab. I'll meet you downstairs."

"You want me to come today?"

"Today, tomorrow, you name it."

"Let's make it tomorrow, then. Around five." Tomorrow was Sunday. Judy would be going to Larchmont or someplace like it to spend the day with her parents. David could slip away from Jake's unobserved.

"Give me a call before you leave," I said. He said he would and thanked me, and we hung up. I sighed.

"You have only yourself to blame," Jackie said from the doorway. "You wanted to run the Antiqua Players. Come eat lunch."

Jackie's eggs were delicious and Jackie's coffee a decided improvement over the strange fluids served at the monastery. After lunch, I dutifully helped clean up the dishes. Then Jackie took her viol into the back bedroom to practice, and I settled down for a solid afternoon with the music from the Queen's book.

Instead of taking each piece in turn, which is what I'd started the week doing, I was working much more selectively. I had already gone through the entire stack of photocopies and had picked out the twenty or so pieces that seemed the best and most interesting for a broken or mixed consort like the Antiqua Players. Some of the pieces were quite short, which meant that there wasn't enough mixed instrumental material for a full-length concert. But I'd left out the solo harpsichord music and the music written in lute tablature. Ralph and David could sort through this, and if each of them did one solo number we'd run just about long enough. If worst came to worst, I told myself, we could always hire a singer and fill in with one or two of the songs for voice and lute. But I didn't want to do it. A singer would be temperamental, and God knows we already had enough temperament on hand. Besides, if the world premiere of the music from Queen Elizabeth's own book—stolen—was going to attract publicity, I wanted the Antiqua Players to grab every single scrap of it.

Elizabethan staff notation turns the eyeballs inside out. For a second, sitting there with a pile of it in front of me, I was tempted to call Music-Rite or one of the other agencies that hire penniless music students to turn musical manuscripts into neatly penned performing scores. After about two more seconds, I junked that idea. Transcribing is expensive. And why take a chance on having a copyist find out too much about this music and where it came from?

Enough of this. I picked up my Number Two pencil and went to work.

By dinnertime, I'd made rough transcriptions of eight of the pieces, including one anonymous four-part fantasia that was like a Chinese crossword puzzle to get into score but that might be a strong centerpiece for a concert or a recording. I was already working out the instrumentation in my head. We'd use bass viol and maybe bass recorder on the bottom line. David could play a tenor viol on the tenor part. The part was fairly easy, which was a good thing, because David is not exactly the Jascha Heifetz of the tenor viol. Anyway, I'd play the alto part, either on flute or on treble viol, and Terry would take the top line on recorder. It would sound juicy, I knew.

My back ached from the deskwork, and my fingers were stiff from wielding a pencil, but I sat back in my chair with a solid sense of satisfaction. Apart from getting through a lot of work, I was pleased about something else. As nothing else could have, the hands-on drudgery had made me understand the music. And it had put my mind in touch with the mind of the person who had set down the music, page by page, in Father Gilmary's book. That person, whoever it was, was no mere copyist. Of this I was certain, and for good reason. In too many of the pieces by well-known composers like Byrd and Farnaby and Dowland, there were changes from what I was used to seeing and playing. Here, the ending might be slightly different. There, a second strain or a division might spiral off in an unusual way. Taken together, these quirks and twists became a kind of handwriting. Squinting at the music, I'd come to recognize it, to enjoy picking up the traces, sometimes faint, sometimes clear, of a distinctive musical style.

I was fairly sure also that the style was a lot like the style of the pretty little piece Jackie and I had tried out the night Morlock had called, the piece we were calling "Eliza's Galiardo."

So, as I straightened up, rubbed my eyes, and stretched to ease the kink in my neck, I felt more than a craftman's sense of accomplishment. I felt oddly moved, as if across the centuries I'd heard an actual voice speaking to me, and speaking in my own language.

Jackie had finished practicing an hour before, and I could hear her singing to herself as she moved around in the kitchen. "Hey," I said to her as I nabbed an apple from the basket on the counter, "do you realize that this is the second meal in a row you're cooking here?"

"I know," Jackie said. "I checked it out with my NOW shop steward and she said it was okay this once. That is, if *you* peel the onions."

"What are we having?" I asked cautiously.

"A pilaf, and it will be delicious. The onions are over there."

"I know where the onions are," I said, "it's my kitchen." I was all set to start peeling when the doorbell rang. I jumped, but it was Ralph. "What gives?" I asked him.

"Not much," he answered, shedding a beautifully tailored white linen jacket. "Maybe a little trouble with a friend."

"You, too, huh?" I told him about David and he laughed.

"Nothing so melodramatic," he said. "I was being a pig because I felt twitchy. So here I am."

"Ralph, is that you?" Jackie called from the kitchen. "Alan has to do onions. Don't distract him."

"I have to do onions," I said.

"Ah," said Ralph. "Domesticity." A moment later, sniffling over the onions, I heard the rattle as Ralph threw back the lid of the harpsichord. A moment after that came pure delight. Ralph, who seldom plays Bach where anybody can hear it—he thinks he's too young to do Bach justice—was playing the "Goldberg Variations" for us.

Ralph is our only gay. I've heard fierce arguments on both sides of the issue, but I've never been able to decide whether or not being gay makes any difference to a musician's music. Ask Ralph and he'll give you his most mocking grin. Tell you one thing, though. Put Ralph Mitchell in a serious mood at a keyboard, and you won't care which sex he favors or from whence in his psyche cometh his inspiration.

I sat there with a half-skinned onion in my hand. Jackie stood in front of the stove. On it, a skillet sizzled and smoked dangerously, but neither of us made a move. We were too busy listening.

"Wow! He's getting *very* expressive," Jackie half-whispered.

"He is," I agreed, "but he's going too fast. Hey!" I twisted in my seat but kept my own voice low. "Slow down a little!" The answer from the studio was a cascade of sixteenth notes in both hands. Ralph almost made it through the passage. Almost. But things were too far out of control, and the virtuoso flight ended in a thump.

"You have definitely earned your dinner," Jackie said when Ralph bounced into the kitchen in search of comment.

"It's amazing, isn't it?" Ralph said. "I'm playing so well. I'm sure it's because I'm not practicing at all."

"Humph," I said, reaching for the last onion.

"By the way . . ." We'd eaten Jackie's pilaf flavored with *my* onions, followed up with a watercress salad and fruit and cheese, and were relaxedly sipping our coffee when Ralph dropped his bombshell.

"I think I was followed on my way over here tonight."

"*Followed?*" I nearly dropped my cup. "Followed by who?"

"Whom," Jackie corrected me calmly.

"Grrr," I said. "Okay, Ralph. *Whom* followed you?"

"I think there were two of them," he said. "Awful-looking types. One of them was wearing a blazer. He had a face like a weasel." It had to be Boddy and Cave.

"What on earth did you do?" Jackie asked.

"Well, at first I thought they were, you know, cruising. But then, they just slunk along after me and didn't try to catch up or anything. So I thought to myself, Goody, goody, muggers." Among his other accomplishments, Ralph lists a judo brown belt, and he intensely dislikes muggers. "I turned a corner and waited for them. But when they saw me, they simply stopped. There we all were, looking at each other."

"Then what?" I said. Ralph gave a kind of giggle.

"I put my hands on my hips and said in my best tart's voice, 'Want something, Ducky?' The one in the blazer was livid."

"Did they do anything?"

"The other one mumbled something, and then they both turned around and hotfooted it away. They looked so silly. After they'd gone and I had time to think, I knew they must be your precious pair."

"Absolutely," I said. "I wonder what they wanted."

"Who cares?" Ralph asked. "They didn't get it."

"Maybe they were just trying to make nuisances of themselves," Jackie suggested.

"You mean, just to let us know they're still around?" I said. "Could be. Cops *do* do that sort of thing."

"And to make you nervous," Ralph said.

"I *am* nervous," I said. "Here we are, going into rehearsal for a concert of Queen Elizabeth's music and we don't have a bit of proof that Queen Elizabeth had anything to do with the music. They can say we faked the whole thing just to get publicity."

"*Christus,*" Jackie said. "I never thought of that."

"Oh, for God's *sake,*" Ralph said impatiently. "Father Gil-What'sit must have some letters or papers or something."

"Gilmary," I said. "And he says he does, but I've never seen them."

"Well, I think you should stop being *morbid.* You saw the book, after all. And all of those other people, Cave and Tarleton Morlock—he's a friend of Boris's, by the way, and Boris says you should have nothing to do with him—and the sexy lady, they're all after the book. So it's not just your say-so."

"True," I admitted, feeling better.

"Well, then."

"Who's Doris?" Jackie asked.

"Not Doris, Boris. Boris de Nagy. He runs the Barn. You've met him at my place." The Barn was Ralph's name for the very superior school of ballet at which he often worked as a *repetiteur,* or accompanist.

"I agree with Boris," I said. "Tarleton Morlock is a wonderful person to stay away from. Boddy and Cave, ditto. Angelica Lederman—"

"Ditto," said Jackie tartly.

"Anybody in the mood for a sonata?" Ralph asked quickly.

"I'd love to go over that Leclair," I said, "the D major."

"Ah, yes," said Ralph, "the one you messed up at the Apple Hollow concert." I shot him a sour look.

"Seeing as we're playing it on Tuesday and again in November, I think a run-through might make sense."

"What you need," Jackie said after we'd played the brisk first movement, "is some long-note practice."

"Thanks," I said. Played by someone who's out of practice, the wooden flute sounds exactly the way a can of ill-mixed tomato soup tastes: watery on top, thick on the bottom. Stirring cures the soup. To cure the flute-playing, you play long notes. That is, you start with the note at the bottom of the register, play it and hold it as long as you can. You do this first without vibrato—the controlled vibration that lends richness to the sound—then with slow vibrato, then with faster vibrato, and so on. After about three notes, your tone will be much better. You will also be breathing deeply if you're in good shape and gasping and glassy-eyed if you're not. Like so many other practice routines, long-note practice is best done far away from the company of others.

Just to please Jackie, I played a few long notes.

"Better," she said judiciously. She was just being nice. In fact, I needed to stop racing around the countryside late at night and to start practicing the flute *and* the violin. I also needed to pay my rent, get my teeth checked, and have the tailor let out my tuxedo trousers.

"We'll do the slow movement now," I said. We did the slow movement. It wasn't much better. My tone was better because I didn't have to concentrate on the fingering of fast passages. But I was thinking so hard about tone that my phrasing went out of whack and the thing sounded oddly disconnected.

"When is this concert?" Ralph asked.

"Tuesday. When I booked it, I had no idea. . . ."

"And today is?"

108

"You know perfectly well. It's Saturday." Ralph sat at the harpsichord. He didn't say anything. He just drummed his fingers on the flat part of the music desk.

"Well," said Jackie brightly after a long pause. "Are we going to try the third movement?" Ralph shrugged. But he flipped the page of his music, got his registrations all set, and looked at me expectantly.

"You start," I said civilly. "So you give us the beat."

"So I do," said Ralph. "Sorry, I'm sure." He gave us a crooked grin and threw us half a bar for free. "Three and four *and*. . . ." His chin dipped slightly in signal, and he was off on his four measures of solo. At the beginning of measure three, Jackie joined him.

"NOW," I said to myself and picked up what I thought was my cue.

"You're late," Ralph said sharply, to make sure we heard over the uproar. Leclair, third movement, ground to a halt.

"I can't be late," I said. Jackie smiled. "Okay, again." Ralph repeated his counting routine, and once again Jackie brought her gamba in absolutely perfectly under the whispery treble of the harpsichord. What a sound! It was sheer pleasure to listen.

"You're late," Ralph said again. He said it with exaggerated patience. I'd listened for a beat too long.

"All *right*," I muttered between my teeth. "One more time." And this time, for some reason, all of the distractions of that day and the day before blew away like smoke, and there were only the three of us and the music. My tone problems disappeared. My fingers, which had been moving like turkey drumsticks, suddenly regained their nimbleness. Everything stayed that way for the rest of the evening and through the Sunday and Monday rehearsals. It stayed that way on Tuesday night, when it rained and we played the Leclair and the rest of the program before a house of about ninety people and the manager's cat at the Hermione and Anton Fink Memorial downtown. The ninety people applauded like mad. The cat nabbed a large mouse backstage at intermission, a feat the manager dismissed airily as commonplace on concert nights. "You should have been here the night he caught a sitar player." I was

109

glad Ralph had missed the bloodshed. Jackie wouldn't have turned a hair, but Ralph's performance nerves were always stretched tight.

Our fee, after deducting half of the cost of printing the programs at the Krazy Kat Kwik Kopy Korner, owner, the manager's brother-in-law, was four hundred eighty-five dollars.

"Never mind," Ralph said consolingly, "you made a tremendous recovery."

"Pass the duck sauce," Terry said.

"How can you put duck sauce on chicken with walnuts?" Ralph asked with a shudder.

"I like duck sauce," Terry said.

I'd added Angelica Lederman's thirty dollars to our fee and had come to the erroneous conclusion, enthusiastically endorsed by all, that we could afford Uncle Weng's. Uncle Weng's has linen tablecloths on all the tables, not just the ones in front, and Uncle Weng in the kitchen when his hay fever allows, but it has not yet been discovered by Mimi Sheraton. We save it for special occasions like this one. As usual when I'd played well, I was ravenous. So were we all.

"Comfort him with duck sauce," I said, "for he is weary with love."

"Me?" said Terry indignantly. "Never."

"Heinz Holliger never eats duck sauce," Jackie said. Heinz Holliger is a very, very good oboist, quite possibly the best in the world. How Heinz Holliger breathes in and blows out at the same time was currently one of Terry's major preoccupations.

"All oboe-players eat duck sauce," Terry said with his mouth full. "Greatest thing in the world for your lip."

It felt great to sit there in Uncle Weng's, stuffed to the brim on chicken with walnuts, Szechuan bean curd, shrimp with hot garlic sauce, and ginger pork, while the rain beat down in torrents on Broadway. I hoped Boddy and Cave and Morlock and Angelica Lederman were all out there in the rain while we sipped hot tea and gossiped about music and the barbed-wire politics of music in New York. I hoped they would stay far away forever.

I cleared my throat. "Listen up, folks."

110

"Speak, O chief!" Ralph intoned.

"When you're hot, you're hot," I said profoundly. "I'd like to start rehearsing the Queen Elizabeth material tomorrow afternoon."

"I can't," Terry said at once, "I have to give a lesson."

"I can't, either," said Jackie.

"Come to think of it," I said, "I have to give a lesson. Okay, tomorrow evening."

"Look here," Ralph said, "why do we always have to call rehearsals that start at ten o'clock at night and last until three in the morning? Let's start at five sharp and break up at a reasonable hour."

"Fine," I said. "If you guys really will show up."

"Okie-dokie by me," Terry said, and Jackie and David agreed. Which explains why things turned out the way they did on Wednesday the whatever-it-was of October.

CHAPTER FOURTEEN

"Bela Lugosi is wearing this *nose*," Ralph said with an expression of manic glee, "and as he begins to reach out, it starts to melt. . . ."

"Okay, okay," I interrupted hastily, "we'll go. Now I know why you wanted to rehearse at five o'clock."

"Heh heh heh," said Ralph, rubbing his hands in an evil way.

"I'm not sure I want to go," Jackie said. "I get scared."

"Me, too," said David, but what he really meant was, "Judy might find me." He'd been living in the small back bedroom since Sunday night and going out as little as possible except for the Tuesday concert and dinner at Uncle Weng's, when we'd been his protection. He swore he could see Judy's mother's Cadillac from his window, double-parked on the side street and waiting in ambush.

"Oh, come on," Ralph said. "You can close your eyes at the horrible parts. And it's absolutely the best popcorn in town."

For once, we'd started and ended a rehearsal on time. Terry had gone off to somebody's loft party, I think in Union City. And now, the other four of us were lined up with monster-movie freaks from all over the West Side for what the Fleapit was billing as a "Pre-Halloween Festival of Frenzy." A dubious Jackie clutched my hand as we bought our tickets and climbed to the balcony, stopping en route for four giant bags of the celebrated popcorn.

112

"It's not so awful," I whispered to Jackie during one graveyard scene, and she nodded agreement and snuggled closer like a teenager. Bela Lugosi's nose did indeed melt, and many screams were screamed and many stakes were driven through black hearts, and by the time we lurched out of the theater, groggy and slightly ill from too much synthetic butter, it was after eleven.

We were on Amsterdam, about a block away from home, when Jackie stopped short and said, "Alan! What if there's . . . somebody . . . in the apartment?" Ralph and I laughed, but David looked uneasy.

"That *would* be Gothic, wouldn't it?" Ralph said.

"Don't worry," I added my own two cents' worth, "If there *is* anybody there, we'll nail him right back in his box."

"Don't *say* things like that!" Jackie said with a shudder, but she was giggling, too. She let us lead the way into the nice bright lobby, if you call a couple of 50-watt bulbs in dirty fixtures bright. "Well," she added as we went up in the elevator, "don't say I didn't warn you."

Like the lobby, the landing and the hallway in front of my apartment seemed utterly normal. That is, chilly, unmopped and smelling slightly of the curries the Chandragors in the rear three-and-a-half cooked and ate at least three times a day. I unlocked the door and snapped on the hall light and we all went into the studio.

"There," I said, "you see? There's nothing—" I stopped dead. Because there wasn't nothing, there was something. Something making soft scuffling noises in the room down the hall.

My bedroom.

"It's Judy," David mumbled. "It's gotta be. I'm getting out of here." He darted out of the room and disappeared.

Jackie stood perfectly still in the center of the studio, turned ashen and gave one small squeak. Ralph and I looked at each other.

"Jackie, listen," I said softly. She paid no attention. "Jackie!" This time, she gulped and nodded. "Go in the kitchen and call the cops! You know, nine-one-one. Hurry!" The kitchen was

113

across the hall and well out of line with the bedroom. Jackie made almost no sound as she tiptoed out of the studio.

The noises stopped.

Again, Ralph and I exchanged glances.

"You want to go back there?" I asked him. He shook his head vehemently. I nodded my agreement. But then, like a moron, I sneaked over to the double doors and peered out into the hall. I think I had some vague idea of making sure Jackie was all right. But the sound I heard next wasn't Jackie.

God!

It was a door being flung savagely open and smacking hard against a wall. The door to my bedroom. I waited, scarcely breathing. Whoever was in there was on his way out. *Or was he?* The thought scared me out of my wits. The slamming door could have been a bluff, couldn't it? Because maybe this wasn't just your common ordinary West Side burglar. Maybe it was someone with a definite target in mind. Someone who wanted me to go up that hall after him. . . .

Well, I was too smart for that. I was going to get out of the studio and into the kitchen and out the service door, taking David, Ralph, and Jackie along, and we were going to wait outside for the cops. Or maybe just run back to the Fleapit for the late show. I turned and gestured to Ralph to follow me. Then I started across the hall.

The sudden rush of footsteps froze me where I stood. I couldn't believe what I saw. A huge figure, clad completely in black, was hurtling down the hall toward me, hands outstretched. *Bela Lugosi,* I thought, then, *no, it's the dancer Merce Cunningham.* But this was more like a football tackle than a dancer. The most appalling thing was, he had no face.

I remember letting out a yell and shrinking back, but I was much too late. A heavy body cannonaded into me, and the impact spun us both back through the studio doors and into the studio itself, and there on the floor I found myself fighting for my life with a bulky, heaving opponent who snarled like an animal as he set at me, and who smelled of his own sweat and, grotesquely, of Royall Lyme cologne.

We scuffled frantically, in a tangle of arms and legs. I could feel my jacket rip as I struggled to get out from under the weight that was pinning me down. The burglar, if that's what he was, was a lot stronger than I was. And cunning as well. At once, he went for my weakest spot.

My hands. The fragile, irreplaceable tools of my craft.

He grabbed at the little finger of my right hand, missed and grabbed again. His own hand was slippery with sweat and I jerked away in time, but he went after the finger again and this time he caught it and was just starting to bend it back when I freed my left hand and struck out with it and clawed at something soft. He grunted and let go of my finger to club furiously at my face, but I had hold of his nose under the fabric of whatever he was wearing over his face, and breakable though they may be, a musician's fingers are strong. I winced as he hit at me, but I didn't let go and I was hurting him and I was savagely glad of it.

Then I sensed rather than saw a burst of bright light above me. I opened my eyes and looked up. There was David's face, staring anxiously down at us, and in David's hand was something that made me giggle hysterically.

Carefully, his face puckering in concentration, David bent over and hit my assailant once, very hard, with the bottle of ketchup from my kitchen refrigerator.

The burglar gave a curious gurgling sigh and immediately went limp.

I had to shove hard to get his dead weight off of me. Dizzy and gasping for breath, I got to my knees. I had to stay there for what seemed like an hour before I could make it to my feet.

With infinite gentleness, David set down the ketchup bottle on the table near the couch.

"Thanks," I panted.

David gave a nod, but didn't say a word.

The burglar lay on his back, breathing loud snoring breaths. He still looked enormous. I could see now that he was wearing a black turtleneck sweater and dark slacks, and that the mask over his head and face had been improvised out of a woman's black stocking or the leg of a pair of tights.

115

Still breathing hard myself, I flexed my fingers cautiously. Jackie was standing with Ralph in the doorway to the hall. She looked decidedly unhappy. I flashed her my best war-hero grin.

"It's okay," I said. "No bones broken, no harm done. At least, not that I can feel. Did you call the cops?"

She nodded.

"Good," I said. "But in case this character comes around before they get here, I think we'd better do something."

"Clothesline. In the kitchen," Jackie said. She ran to get it.

It's surprisingly hard to truss up a large, unconscious body. Its limbs and head weigh a ton. The arms, in particular, tend to flop awkwardly out of position, and none of us felt happy about cradling the burglar's lolling head to keep from doing it more damage. But we finally did manage to get the hands tied tightly. Then we wound enough turns of rope around the legs to immobilize them without causing gangrene.

We dragged our victim over to the biggest and most battered of my armchairs and propped him in it more or less upright.

"I wonder who he is," Ralph said.

"I know who it is," I said tiredly. I didn't want to touch him any more, but I made myself pluck at the stocking over the burglar's face and pull it clear. I was right. As the mask came away, the balding head and long lantern jaw of Tarleton Morlock emerged.

"But why on earth . . . ?" said Jackie, mystified, when I told her who it was.

"You've got me," I said. "But it looks as if we'll have a chance to find out." Twice as we were talking, Morlock's eyes fluttered open under his sparse, rufous eyebrows. His breathing grew more regular. After a few more seconds, his eyes flickered open again and stayed open.

"Oh-h-h-h," he groaned. "What hit me?"

"Divine retribution," I said. "In the form of a bottle of Heinz's finest ketchup. You know, the stuff the Reagan people say is a vegetable."

Morlock shut his eyes and groaned again, rustily. I was relieved to see that color was returning to his face. His freckles no longer

116

stood out like splotches of brown ink on parchment. He tried to get a hand up to his head. When he realized his hands were tied, his eyes flew wide open and blazed with fury. "You little *fucks*," he said wildly to Ralph and me. "Let me go!"

"When the cops come," I said. "Then we'll let you go."

"Shit," Morlock muttered. The anger was helping him get back his strength, but he was a long way from being Superman. After a minute he said sullenly, "My head is killing me."

"Such a shame," David said.

"What do you think?" I asked Jackie. "Should we get Mr. Morlock an aspirin?"

"Oh, God, yes," said Morlock. He even added, "Please."

"I'll fetch it," Ralph said and left the room. While he was gone, Morlock didn't do any moving or talking. I guess his head really was hurting him.

Ralph came back into the studio. "I found some," he said. "I also found this. On the floor by your bedroom door." He and Jackie fed Morlock a couple of aspirin tablets and some sips of water, while I looked at what Ralph had just handed me. It was a roll-up case of soft brown glove leather, tied shut with short bits of ribbon. I untied it. Inside, in separate stitched pockets, were various implements. Some were familiar—pliers, screwdrivers, a small hammer, a useful-looking chisel. But one or two definitely did not belong in the gentleman's handy home tool kit. For instance, a small but sturdy chromium-plated pry bar. And a cylindrical gadget with a couple of knurled adjustment screws that I knew from reading detective stories had to be a picklock. When Morlock went out on a foray, he not only dressed the part, he carried the right equipment.

I was very careful not to leave any of my fingerprints on Morlock's shiny do-it-yourself hardware.

Morlock watched out of bloodshot eyes as I rolled up the case and tossed it back to Ralph.

"Put it back where I found it?" Ralph asked.

"Exactly. Let's let the cops find it."

"*Shit,*" Morlock said again, this time with real fervor. For quite a while, we all sat quietly, wrapped, as they say, in our own

117

thoughts. Then Morlock broke the silence. "Well," he said sarcastically, "I suppose you think you're pretty good, catching the big fierce robber?"

Jackie looked at him thoughtfully. "I have a little cousin just like you," she said. "He steals things. And every time they catch him, he cries the same way you do."

"Ho, ho, very funny," Morlock said. But he flushed brick-red when he said it.

"What I want to know," I said, "is what the big fierce robber was doing here in the first place."

Morlock looked at me incredulously. "Why, you know what I came for," he said. "I came to have a look at that manuscript of yours."

I raised my eyebrows. "A look?"

"Maybe more than a look." Morlock wriggled in his bonds. "God's sake, man," he said fretfully, "I spent a whole damned lunch warning you about what might happen. And by the Lord Harry, I was right! A ten-year-old boy could have gotten in here and pillaged the place."

I stared at him, amazed. Even though I knew from past experience what Tarleton Morlock was like, I had trouble believing my ears. "The next thing you'll be telling me," I said, "is that you were only robbing me for my own good."

Morlock shrugged awkwardly. "Well. You don't expect me to philosophize, do you, under these circumstances?" He glanced down at the rope on his wrists. "But what the hell. The way I see it, if you haven't got the sense to keep a beautiful thing safe, you've got to expect that somebody else will try to take it off you. And frankly, they'll be doing you a favor."

"Wow," Jackie breathed.

"What's 'wow,' young lady?" Morlock demanded. "Haven't you ever met an honest man before?"

"A psychopath, you mean," Jackie said.

Morlock smirked. "I've been called that, too," he said complacently.

"Whatever you've been called," I said, "I can't understand why you'd run the risk of getting caught like this just to have a look at

118

something, or even steal something, worth only a few thousand dollars."

"Who said that manuscript was only worth a few thousand dollars?"

"You did," I said. "You told me, maybe six or seven thousand."

Morlock laughed out loud. "I did say that, didn't I?" he said. "And you were stupid enough to believe me. Incredible." He shook his head gingerly. "Ouch. I told you that to put you off guard, so you wouldn't bother to protect it." He smirked again. "My little ploy worked, didn't it?"

"Not quite," I said.

"Well, maybe not all the way," he said.

"Jackie, how long before the cops get here?"

"They said they'd put the complaint on the air right away," Jackie said.

"There you go," I said to Morlock. "Any minute, the police will arrive. And when they do, you're in the soup up to your ears."

"Really?" Morlock drawled. He sounded bored.

"Yes, really," I said. "Burglary, breaking and entering, felonious assault, possession of burglar's tools. . . ."

"Why must you be so stupid?" Morlock said. "You'll never make any of those charges stick."

"What are you talking about?" I said. "I have witnesses." Morlock snorted.

"Your girl friend and some other friends of yours," he said disdainfully. "Nobody's going to believe *them*. Now, you listen and I'll tell you exactly what I'll say to the cops if they ever do show up. First, I didn't just come over here on the spur of the moment. You *invited* me here. My secretary's got it written down in her appointment book. When I arrived, you were out. I waited outside for a while and when you didn't answer your doorbell, I tried the door and it was unlocked."

"I locked it," I said. "I always lock it."

"Try and prove it," Morlock said. "Anyway, when I discovered that the door was unlocked I felt nervous. We'd been discussing the possibility of your being burgled and now maybe you *were*

119

being burgled. So I went in, somewhat cautiously, I must admit. And what did I find?"

"A Daddy chair, a Mommy chair, and a Baby chair?" I asked.

"I wouldn't try to be funny with the police if I were you," Morlock said. "No. On the bedroom floor, I found a roll of tools—"

"With your fingerprints all over them," I interrupted.

"Naturally," Morlock shot back. "I was curious, so I examined them. But I'd never seen them before, and you can't prove I had. Anyway, I was about to make sure nothing was missing, especially the precious manuscript that you'd already told me was carelessly safeguarded—"

"I never told you anything," I said.

"—when I heard you come in. Ah, I thought, I'll just trot down the hall and explain things. And then . . . instead of thanking me, you grab me and wrestle with me and this thug here—" he jerked his chin at Ralph, who bowed politely "—hits me over the head. With a ketchup bottle," he added aggrievedly. "At least you could have used a bottle of cognac."

Not ten minutes earlier, this monster had been doing his best to destroy me. He was obviously obsessed with beautiful things, and never mind about people. But . . . cognac instead of ketchup! I'll say this for the monster, he had style. Despite everything, I found myself laughing, and Jackie and Ralph were laughing, too. "You're unbelievable," I said.

"Not in the least," Morlock answered. "I'm extremely believable. Far more so, my friend, than you are. You realize that this whole business will be my word against yours, and I'm a former curator at the Met and on the boards of half a dozen places. And you—you're nobody. A run-of-the-mill nobody at that. A hungry musician with a lucky find who wants some free publicity. That's what you are, and that's why the wild accusations against me."

Lose your temper against someone as cold and smart as Morlock and you're cooked. "My gosh," I said with what I hoped was aplomb. "You paint such a flattering picture. Instead of turning you over to the cops, I'm tempted to do something nice. Like smearing you with maple syrup and staking you out over an anthill."

But Morlock was already shifting gears. "Good Lord, Alan," he said earnestly. "I don't for a minute feel like saying such awful things about you. I'm just trying to point out to you and your friends how things will develop if the police do arrive and find me like this."

"Not that I really want to know," I said, "but what do you suggest?"

"Release me," Morlock said commandingly. "Release me at once and I'll say nothing more about this whole unfortunate business."

Ralph's jaw dropped, and then he laughed. Jackie looked first at Morlock, then at me and then, longingly, at the bottle of ketchup.

"Let's all relax," I said. "I've got a better idea."

"Let's hear it by all means," Morlock said. "But remember, we may not have much time."

"Oh, there's plenty of time," I said. "I think we should call the newspapers. And maybe the TV people, too. If we're looking for publicity, now's the chance to get some. Besides, we tell our story first." Never mind that our story would be somewhat *complicated* by the fact that we didn't have the priceless manuscript that all the fuss was about.

"Definitely the TV networks," Ralph said, grinning. Morlock, whatever he was actually thinking, permitted himself to express no more than mild concern.

"I'd have to disagree with that," he said, as calmly as if we were all at his club sipping martinis and debating some fine point of backgammon play. "If you call in the press, I assure you you'll get yourselves in much worse trouble. The police won't be terribly amused, and of course I won't be, either. Besides . . ." he smiled the kind of smile that Reynard the Fox reserves for his U.S.D.A. Extra Fancy friends ". . . don't you have a great deal more to gain if I'm on your side?"

At last.

"I've been hoping you'd ask that question," I said, smiling an even broader smile. "You've broken in here and damn near killed me. Tell us how you could possibly be on our side."

"Well, for one thing," Morlock said, "if your manuscript is okay I could pay you a great deal of money for it."

"Sounds promising," I said. "How much this time?" We waited, fascinated, while the wheels went around in Morlock's head.

"Oh . . . maybe half a mil or so," he said, watching me to savor the greed in my eyes. I shook my head.

"Sorry," I said. Angelica Lederman had been talking about a million and a half.

"Now, look, goddammit," Morlock said. "You can't expect me to quote you anything serious when I've never even seen the manuscript and you've got me bound hand and foot besides. Take off these bloody ropes and maybe we can review the bidding together like civilized men."

"Jackie," I said, "you know where I keep the Polaroid?" Jackie nodded. She and Ralph broke into understanding smiles. "You've talked me into it," I said to Morlock. "I'm going to let you go. *And* I'm going to give you one more chance to become the lucky owner of a wonderful manuscript. But first, I think I'm entitled to a little insurance." I moved around the room, snapping pictures of Morlock with the Polaroid. I took eight in all, a full roll. Some showed Morlock full-face without his stocking mask. For a couple, we pulled the mask back on. In the best one, the open case of burglar's tools was propped in Morlock's lap. But they all were perfectly identifiable.

After I finished my picture-taking, I sat down at the table and did some writing with a marker pen on the backs of the pictures. Then I went back over to Morlock. "Are you right-handed or left-handed?"

"Right-handed. Why?"

"Because you're going to sign and date the backs of these pictures. They all say the same thing: 'Taken on the night I broke into Alan French's studio.'"

This time, the Morlock grin was more of a rictus. "You know I can't put my signature on anything like that!" he said.

"Ralph, do I hear someone in the hall? Someone in blue?" Morlock froze.

"All right," he said sullenly, "you win." Carefully, we freed his

122

right hand enough to let him write, and he signed all of the photographs. Then we untied him the rest of the way.

"There's no use your trying to steal these," I said, putting the photographs into an envelope. "First thing in the morning, they're going into my safe-deposit box along with my father's fraternity pin and my great-aunt's best cameo brooch." Morlock rubbed his wrists to ease the soreness and got gingerly to his feet. He grimaced and lowered himself back onto the chair.

"God, my poor old noggin!" he said. "It's what you get, I suppose, for trying to relive your fraternity days."

"No hurry," I said magnanimously, "take your time."

"Well," Morlock said after he'd recovered himself, "now that we're friends, aren't you going to give me a look at the manuscript?"

"Not yet, old friend," I said, "but don't worry. You are an honored customer. In the next couple of days, I'll call you up and make a date, and you can come and look it over to your heart's content." And God forgive me for telling such a thumping great lie.

Morlock wanted to argue about the delay. But his aching head and his need to be gone by the time the cops arrived somewhat weakened his argument. In the end, I had to help him downstairs and into a taxi. "Christ," he groaned as he slumped in the seat, "you play rough on the West Side."

About half an hour later, the doorbell rang. It was the police, represented by two tired-looking detectives. We'd made up a story about having locked the burglar in a bathroom only to have him break out and escape through the service entrance. But the cops didn't even ask us what happened. As soon as we told them that nothing was missing, they shut up their notebooks and got ready to leave.

"What took you guys so long to get here?" I asked them as we waited for the elevator. The thin-faced one with the widow's peak consulted his notes.

"We caught the beep at eleven-seventeen. At eleven-twenty-two, we got word of a mugging on Ninety-eighth. The old lady was still alive, so we had to try to take her statement. At eleven-

123

fifty, we received word that a man had shot his wife on Ninety-first and Riverside. Turns out he only nicked her."

"Yeah, just a few birdshot in the leg," said the second cop.

"Still, we had to hold him until the jocks from the precinct got there," said the first cop. "It all takes time, ya know? Anyway, we were headed over here when we caught another beep. Twelve-twenty. A lady on a hundred and third street, bee-and-ee. They cleaned the place out, took everything. Including her pet canary."

"Her *canary*?" I said.

"So that's why it took us over an hour to get here," the first cop went on. "One mugging, one attempted murder, one burglary."

"I can't believe they'd take a canary," I said.

"Hey, be careful, you canary-owners," said the second cop as the elevator arrived. "It's a jungle out there."

Plato and Aristotle . . . considered this (Phrygian Mode) intense, vehement, violent, and very severe and capable of astonishing people . . . . The subject of frightful wars lends itself to this manner.
                    Nicholas Poussin, Letter to Chantelou,
                         November 24, 1647

CHAPTER FIFTEEN

By comparison with Wednesday night, Thursday was as placid as a millpond. Jackie, Ralph, and I were up till all hours talking about Morlock, so naturally we slept late on Thursday morning. On my way out to the deli for the raw materials of brunch, I spotted Sergeant Boddy keeping lonely vigil at a table in Nino's. On my way back, armed with two pounds of ham, a quarter-pound of smoked salmon, a dozen fat hot dogs, two packages of cream cheese, and two dozen bagels, I stopped to peer into a store window. Reflected in the glass was Inspector Cave, pretending not to be inspecting me from a doorway across the street. But apart from watching, neither Boddy and Cave nor anybody else actually did anything.

Terry and David, back from Union City, came by about noon. We ate a vast and delicious brunch, spent the afternoon rehearsing, and finished up around seven o'clock. After the others had gone—David was now seeing somebody in Union City—Jackie and I had soup for dinner, which was very soothing, and found time at last for a few tender moments together, which was even more soothing. The only interruption of this idyll was a phone call from Father Gilmary. No, there was no news of any kind about the manuscript. But we'd be pleased to know that Brother Simon had been pronounced recovered and released from the hospital, and was back on duty at the monastery. I wasn't sure exactly how pleased I was, Brother Simon being one of my least favorite monks, but I said something polite to Father Gilmary and promised to call him the next afternoon.

At seven-fifty-two the next morning by my bedside digital clock, the phone rang once again. I knew I shouldn't answer it. But I had no idea of the size of the tsunami that was about to crash on our little island of tranquillity.

"Alan? Alan French?" Jackie murmured something and rolled over onto her side of the bed as I tried to figure out whose girlish voice was daring to pipe in my ear at that hour. "Alan, this is Melanie."

Melanie?

"You know, Melanie the Artist Liaison Person. From Apple Hollow."

Oh. Yeah. Melanie.

"You're not mad? That I'm calling so early?" I scratched my head and grunted something into the receiver. "Oh, I'm so glad. But probably you want to know what this is all about."

"Well, Apple Hollow is having a benefit auction. To raise money, because Mrs. Smerdnikoff the principal says we're flat broke."

Don't believe Mrs. Smerdnikoff, Melanie. She's got the dough hidden away somewhere. Maybe in the barn.

"So we're giving this auction and I thought you might like to come. It's this afternoon at Ezekiel's, that's on Route Seven—"

All of a sudden, a bell was ringing loudly in my head and amber lights were flashing and I wasn't groggy any more. "Melanie, did you say—"

"Ezekiel's, that's right. It's an auction gallery. On Route Seven about ten miles north—"

"Listen, Melanie," I gabbled, "I can't talk now but I'm coming, we're coming. Route Seven?"

"Oh, that's wonderful. Smerdy will be so pleased. On Route Seven." I could hear that huge dog of hers woofing away companionably as she gave me directions. "Be *quiet*, Newton. His name's Fig Newton, Newton for short. Now, two-thirty. Don't forget."

126

Two-thirty. Oh, my God.

I'll never know how we did it. Actually, I *do* know: It was Jackie. It was Jackie who remembered that Ralph was getting up early to practice. Who thought of having Ralph pick up the rental car and then pick us up. Who even brewed a pot of fresh coffee, put it in a Thermos, and turned the ruins of yesterday's brunch into sandwiches for three. Meanwhile, I threw on clothes and brooded about being late and debated whether or not to call Father Gilmary with the news and decided it was better to wait.

And at noontime, we were standing at the doorway to the monastery, breathing in the crisp air of a beauty of a fall day, listening to a pair of chickadees argue in a shadbush and waiting for Brother Simon to spoil it all.

As usual, he took his time answering the door. And as usual, he cackled evilly when he saw visitors. "Hee, heee, hee! Don't tell me, I never forget a face. It's Mister French. And his lady friend, God defend us against all such. And you, too!" he said to Ralph with a mean smile. "Stop wasting God's time, then, and come in. I'll tell Father you're here." The only change I noticed in Brother Simon as he stumped away was that he'd exchanged his bedroom slippers for a pair of villainous, dirty white tennis sneakers.

Father Gilmary's smile of welcome gave way to surprise when I asked him to get hold of Brother Simon again right away. But as pressed for time as we were, I knew it would be useless to try to hurry the miserable old curmudgeon. So when we were all assembled in the library, with tea and mint chocolate chip cookies in ample supply, courtesy of Brother Martin, I began by congratulating Brother Simon on his recovery.

"Ah, well, there's those as wish I was still in the hospital," he grumbled, scratching himself with vigor.

"You mean, the person who put you there?"

"Him and others, too."

"Well, I'm not one of them," I said with a display of sympathy, but the old devil glowered at me as if he didn't believe a word of it. He was right, of course, but I ignored his black looks and, as slowly and patiently as I could, I took him through his version of what had happened on the day of his misadventure. It was like pulling teeth. But as the minutes ticked by, I grew surer and surer that when Brother Simon shook his head or grunted a monosyllable in answer to a question, he wasn't just being obnoxious. He had something to hide.

"You say you were cleaning when this car drove up," I said.

"Yuh."

"What kind of cleaning were you doing?"

"Just cleaning, that's all. Picking up."

"Bundling things together?"

"Yuh."

"What sorts of things?"

"Unh. All sorts. Junk. Magazines. Old papers."

"What were you going to do with it?"

"With what?"

"The magazines."

"What do you think? Get rid of them."

"Where?" I asked him.

He hesitated, hunching down deeper in his chair.

"Take 'em to the dump. Some of 'em."

"What about the rest of them?"

"I dunno." Then, after a silence, "Maybe sell 'em."

"Sell them? You had somebody who wanted to buy old magazines?"

"Fella down the road. Wanted old stuff from the attic."

"Did you ever sell him anything else?"

"Nah. I never sold him that old book! You can't prove nothing about that book!" Brother Simon gesticulated frantically, then pointed a shaky finger at me. "I'm not saying a word about that book!"

Father Gilmary looked at him. "I'm afraid you must, Brother," he said, "even if you don't want to." His voice was gentle, his authority absolute.

Bit by bit, he got the story out of the old man. About how the arrival from England of Father Gilmary and Brother Martin had disrupted his life in the monastery and had made more work for Brother Simon. ("The damn telephone going off day and night, and me the only one to run after it.") About Brother Simon's little arrangement with the man from Ezekiel's, who would come up in a pickup to take away the stuff Brother Simon dragged down from the attic—bushels of stuff, some of it dating back to the days before the place had been a monastery. About the small sums that changed hands, and the occasional case of Brother Simon's favorite beer.

Brother Simon had in fact been cleaning the morning of the day he had been knocked out. The man from Ezekiel's had driven up looking for another bargain load, and Brother Simon had had an inspiration. "Let him take the damn book away with him, and that'll be an end of it." So Brother Simon had gone up to the library. The book was locked inside its steel box, but "I knew where Father kept the key." And so, Queen Elizabeth's priceless music-book had been dumped unceremoniously into a cardboard carton along with a pile of old magazines and carted off to Ezekiel's Auction Gallery. The man from Ezekiel's had paid extra on account of the book. He'd given Brother Simon five dollars.

"Merciful Mary," prayed Brother Martin, "please let the book still be there." Father Gilmary's lips moved in a silent "Amen."

After the man had driven away with his load, Brother Simon had become frightened about what he'd done. Then he'd heard the returning Volkswagen. Half in remorse, half in calculation, he'd picked up a sharp stone from the garden in front of the house and whacked himself on the temple. He hadn't knocked himself out, of course, but he'd hit himself hard enough to draw blood ("there I was bleeding like a stuck pig and no one to help me") and to be convincingly groggy—and scared—when Brother Martin and Father Gilmary found him.

"And, by God!" Brother Simon said when he'd told us the whole sorry tale, "what the devil I did it all for, I wish I knew. Things will never be the same around here again."

"So there's your big mystery," Ralph said.

I looked at my watch. One o'clock. "We've got an hour and a half to get there and find the thing."

"What are we waiting for?" said Brother Martin.

The first thing I saw, or rather felt, when I got out of the car at

Ezekiel's was Fig Newton. "How neat! He remembers you!" Melanie squeaked as the huge brown creature put his forepaws on my shoulders and slurped my face with an affectionate pink tongue.

"Hi, Melanie," I said weakly.

"Hi. *Down*, Newton! Get down!" Newton dropped reluctantly to all fours, his tail waving a *maestoso* beat. "I'm really sorry, Mr. French. He knows he shouldn't."

"That's okay. But Melanie, listen to me. We've got a problem. Will you help?"

"Sure . . . anything." There were absolutely no flies on Melanie. She watched me alertly as I explained. Somewhere inside the big shed that housed Ezekiel's, I told her, possibly in a pile of magazines or used books, there was one book that had gotten there by mistake. A very old book. We had to find it before the auction began. Melanie's eyes widened. "Why, is it valuable?"

"We've got twenty-five minutes," I said, "and, yes, it's valuable. Find it and you'll be in the middle of a tremendous story."

"Super!" she said with a grin. "What I'll do first is talk to some of the kids from school who've been here arranging stuff for the auction."

"Fine," I said. "The cover is blue with gold flowers stamped on it. And listen . . . other people may be looking for it, too. So if you spot it, come and tell me. Or tell Jackie Craine or Father Gilmary here or Brother Martin. But whatever you do, *don't tell anybody else.*"

"I won't," she vowed.

"We'll be inside," I said, "but I'll meet you by the door as soon as the auction begins if we don't see each other sooner." She nodded and ran off to confer with her friends. Newton gave me a fond look and followed her, and we went in the door.

Ezekiel's *was* big. At that moment, it looked to me as big as a hangar for 747s. And of course it was packed solid with merchandise. There was a cleared area where seats were set up in front of a podium for the auctioneer. But the stuff was jammed in everywhere else except in the narrow aisles. And all over the place, on chairs, on tables, atop dressers, inside dingy glass-fronted cabinets, overflowing rickety shelves, were books and magazines by the thousand.

There were people everywhere, too, behaving in the lunatic way people do behave at auctions: stopping abruptly to peer at some bit of shiny metal or chinaware; pressing in vain on the keys of an old melodeon; blocking traffic for minutes on end as they got down stiffly on hands and knees to examine ancient-looking chairs for saw marks and wooden dowels.

"Excuse me," I said, stepping over one recumbent patron.

"Excuse *me*," sniffed an elderly lady with no chin as I squeezed past. The vase she was cradling defensively in her arms still haunts my memory. It looked as if it had been quarried from the world's hugest Alka-Seltzer bottle.

"Sorry," I moaned. Another elderly lady fixed me in a basilisk stare while the steel tip of her spike heel, ground needle-sharp just for this occasion, dug agonizingly into my right instep. Every so often, I caught sight of Jackie, Ralph, and the two men of the cloth, undergoing similar punishment as they kept up the search.

And we weren't the only hunters.

As I pushed my way slowly along an aisle, I suddenly saw, or thought I saw, a familiar profile. Angelica? If it was Angelica, had she seen me? I quickly reversed direction, in too much of a hurry to double check. But while I was wondering how Angelica Lederman had found out about Ezekiel's, and dodging traffic and trying to spot our missing treasure, I saw someone else to make me want to hide in the crowd. This time, there was no question. Sergeant Boddy was standing near the entrance. He was making no effort to join the scrimmage. He simply watched quietly, like a herdsman watching cattle mill around their feed trough. Farmer MacGregor himself. And I was Peter Rabbit.

All at once, my heart jumped. I forgot all about Boddy and the profile that might be Angelica's. *Over there, on that table, a book with a vivid blue cover.* I'd found it! Furtively, I edged over and reached out a hand. My fingers closed on a worn leather binding. . . .

Hans Brinker or The Silver Skates, by Mary Mapes Dodge. One set teethmarks (small) on front cover; one stain, probably chocolate, on title page. Otherwise, excellent. Cursing, I consigned Hans Brinker and all associated with him to the bottom of the Leyden Canal. I was so disappointed that it took me seconds to notice that someone was tugging at my sleeve.

"It's *okay,*" Melanie said, "it's me. We've got it." Oh, sure. I let her pull me through the throng, refusing to believe for one minute that this child and her friends really had found the manuscript. "There," Melanie said matter-of-factly, "in that box."

And there it was, on top of a pile of *Life* magazines, fleurs-de-lis and all. "Wow," I said with sparkling originality. "Jesus." Once again, I reached out. . . .

"Sir! SIR!"

"What's the matter?" I said. A small man in baggy pants, a checked shirt, and a powder-blue sleeveless sweater materialized out of the crowd. On his chest was a badge. "EZEKIEL'S," it read.

"We're starting," the small man said. "No more handling of merchandise." Sure enough, people were filing into the rows of seats near the podium.

"It's okay," I said with what I thought was a winning smile. "I'm buying this book."

"That's part of Lot Eleven," the small man said, stooping to read the label on the carton. "You'll have your chance to bid on it in just about ten minutes."

"But I want to buy it *now,*" I said.

"I'm sorry, Mister, you're too late for a direct purchase." And before I could stop him, the officious little bastard had scooped up the box and carried it off to the area behind the auctioneer's stand.

"Oh, *no,*" Melanie groaned.

"I'm afraid, oh, *yes.*" For a second, I was tempted to charge off after my pint-sized nemesis. But the house was quieting down as people took seats. If I did go after the manuscript, I'd be making myself as conspicuous as I'd be on the stage of Carnegie Hall. Boddy and Angelica—if it *was* Angelica—and God knew who else besides would be watching my every move, and there would be absolutely no place to hide.

Of course, if I didn't go after the manuscript. . . . In desperation, I looked around to see if anyone in our party was near enough to consult. Nobody. Jackie and Ralph were sitting together toward the front. I couldn't find Father Gilmary or Brother Martin at all. Boddy, too, seemed to have vanished, but the fact gave me no comfort.

"What are we going to do?" Melanie asked.

I shrugged.

"What *can* we do?" I said. "We'll have to wait and bid on the box when it comes up." Suddenly, I panicked. I was carrying about thirty-five dollars. The manuscript apart, the magazines and other stuff in that carton looked almost worthless. I couldn't believe that a few dollars wouldn't be enough to make me the lucky owner of Lot Eleven. But what if I was wrong?

Bang! The auctioneer's hammer came down and the auctioneer himself, chunky and dark-haired and wearing a straw us-folks cowboy hat, began to jolly up the crowd.

"See if you can find out whether they take checks here," I whispered to Melanie.

"Okay," she said with that kid-sister squeak in her voice and started to slip through the crowd.

"And see if they've got a listing of the lots," I called after her. The people around stared curiously at me, wondering what sort of oddball would come to an auction without even knowing what was on sale. A lad in a snappy sateen warmup jacket took pity on me and held out a mimeographed list. "Thanks." Lot Eleven was described simply as "a collection of great old wartime picture magazines and an old book."

By the time Melanie wriggled her way back to my side, the auctioneer had ended his spiel and was hard at work on Lot One, which looked vaguely like a bentwood coat rack but was only three feet high. While I was still puzzling over what it could be, it went for twelve dollars to a white-haired citizen on my left.

"Old Salter," said somebody, "he'll slap a top on it and sell it for a lamp stand right out of his barn. He's damn smart."

"No checks," Melanie said, "but they do take American Express."

133

"No got," I said. "How about Visa or MasterCard?" Melanie slipped off again.

Lot Two was a painting of exceptional size and hideousness. It took two attendants to hold the thing up while the auctioneer proclaimed its many virtues. One of them, visibly sweating under the weight of the massive carved-oak frame, was the little guy who had snatched away the manuscript. I wished him no particular harm other than that a murrain might fall upon his cattle and that the painting, frame and all, would drop right on his toe. Somebody who must have had an enormous hole to patch in his roof bought the painting for forty dollars.

"They do take MasterCard," Melanie said, "and here's a catalogue."

"I love you, Melanie," I said distractedly, watching as a wicker sarcophagus sold for six dollars to the lad in the sateen jacket.

"I am promised to another," Melanie said gravely, "but thank you. That boy shouldn't have bought that willow thing."

"Maybe he's planning to live in it," I said, "I've heard there's a serious rural housing shortage."

"Drafty in winter," Melanie said judiciously. "He probably wants it for his motorcycle."

The auctioneer disposed smoothly of Lots Four through Eight, at prices that gave me no reason to be afraid of being outbidden. Lot Nine was another story. Lot Nine was a gargantuan piece of furniture, clearly meant for Glumdalclitch's bedroom. Size apart, Lot Nine was impressive for its complexity. It had drawers and shelves and doors that opened on more shelves. It had a beveled mirror, now somewhat oxidized, that swiveled, swung, and turned. There were little saucer-shaped platforms on which to set candlesticks or bottles of beer. Part of Lot Nine tipped upward, counterbalanced on springs strong enough to absorb the shock of the Tokyo earthquake, though to what purpose I haven't the faintest idea. And Lot Nine caused a bit of a sensation. The crowd murmured when it made its appearance, borne by no fewer than four attendants, and the first bid was a respectable sixty dollars.

The auctioneer looked reproachful. "Folks," he said, "let's get serious." It took him quite a while, but finally he got the bidding going briskly among three parties and knocked it down to a man with fuzzy white hair and an Irish tweed hat—"Obviously a New Yorker," Melanie observed with scorn—for four hundred dollars.

Lot Ten was the melodeon. As jittery as I was, I caught myself admiring the looks of the unplayable old instrument. If I were running a restaurant, one with lots of exposed brick in the walls and lots of carrots in the salad, I'd want something exactly like it for my ivy. The audience was warming up. Somebody in it shared my affection for limed oak and yellowed ivory and had two hundred dollars to spare besides.

And as my nerves started to quiver, out trotted the small man in the blue cardigan with Lot Eleven.

"Friends," said the auctioneer, "this is a boxful of memories." Whoa, I said to myself, easy on the salesmanship. The man pushed his straw hat back from his forehead, reached into the carton and pulled out an old, old *Life* magazine. He held it up to let us all see that it had a wounded GI on the cover. "Some of you won't remember," he said in a rich voice, "but some of you will. What do you bid for a whole pile of our past?"

Nobody said a word.

Then a voice spoke from somewhere in the crowd. "My first husband died on one a them beaches," it said firmly. "Four dollars."

I was just clearing my throat to bid when a terrible thought struck me. The instant I spoke up, everybody in the place would know I was bidding. Everybody, including Angelica and Sergeant Boddy. *And the two of them would know why.*

"I hear four dollars," said the auctioneer. Frantically, I looked everywhere. Then inspiration struck. Thank you, God, I breathed, and nudged Melanie. "Bid five dollars," I whispered.

"Five dollars," Melanie said squeakily.

"Six dollars," said the voice. I winked at Melanie.

"Seven," she said. I was starting to sweat.

"Goddammit," the voice said, "I bid ten dollars." I craned my neck, trying to identify my antagonist.

"Going . . . going . . ." chanted the auctioneer.

"Bid twelve," I whispered.

135

"Twelve dollars," Melanie said obediently.

"You have no heart," the voice said. "Fourteen dollars."

"That's right! Let the lady have the box," somebody else said hoarsely from across the hall.

We bid sixteen dollars.

"Aw-w," said my heckler.

"Now, Joe," the auctioneer said.

"I bid eighteen dollars," my opponent called triumphantly. This time, I was able to spot her in the crowd. I stared at her, appalled. She was at least six feet tall, with arms and shoulders as massive as a man's, but it wasn't her bulk that frightened me. It was partly her face, which was broad and smiling and filled with violence. And then there was her hair. She wore it in a bun, and it was the same yellowish white as the keys of the melodeon. For some reason, this set my teeth on edge. But worst of all was her clothing. She wore a sweater and a conventional print housedress—conventional, except that on so big a woman the dress lost all definition and looked like a tent. Then, under the wide skirt, she had on a man's dark blue dress trousers and heavy black brogues. The effect was obscene.

She stood there, unable to keep still, rocking rhythmically back and forth on her heels, her face still set in an excited smile. She looked like nothing human.

"It's against you, Miss," the auctioneer said to Melanie.

"Let's end it," I said to Melanie. "Bid twenty-five." She did.

"Ah, no you don't," the woman said in her terrible mannish voice, "Thirty!"

"Good for you, lady!" came the thick voice of my heckler.

"Joe, I'm not going to warn you again," the auctioneer said. "And Selma, that's too much money for you to be spending on a box of old magazines. You'd better stop." He looked at Melanie standing beside me. "You want to bid again, Miss?"

"Thirty-five dollars," Melanie said at my behest. Immediately, the auctioneer brought down his hammer.

"Sold," he said, "to the young lady on the side here, for thirty-five dollars, and a good thing, too, Selma."

With Melanie at my heels, I hurried forward to claim my purchase. Some helpful hand had stuffed the book well down into the box, but it was there, all right. I started to grab for it, then made myself move slowly and deliberately to ease it out. There was no time to examine it closely, but it seemed unharmed.

As I handed the cashier my MasterCard, I could hear that unbearable voice raised in outrage. By the time the girl had finished and I'd signed the charge slip and gotten back my card, the voice was yelling almost in my ear. Hastily, I wrapped Queen Eliza in *The Saturday Evening Post* of September 9, 1943, and begged a rubber band from the cashier to snap around the parcel. Then I turned to face my fair underbidder. "I know your kind!" she was saying to me. The fist she was shaking as she said it was the size of a softball. "You think you can come up here and buy anything—"

"Here," I said. I thrust the carton at her and spun on my heel away from her, Eliza tucked firmly under one arm. The yelling stopped as if by magic. While the huge woman gaped at me, I headed for the exit. But Selma was not my only pursuer. Ahead of me, Sergeant Boddy shoved purposefully through the aisles. He'd seen me at last: that much was obvious. Worse, he was moving to cut me off and to judge from the expression on his face, he was looking forward to the encounter.

*[Players] are often found whose ready fingers serve
them well in loud runs, but . . . in the soft ones . . .
they grow nervous, speed onward, and lose control.*
Carl Philipp Emmanuel Bach, On the
True Art of Playing Keyboard
Instruments (1753), p. 149

CHAPTER SIXTEEN

"This way! Hurry!" Angelica Lederman, I was positive,
could never really look upset. But when she caught me by the arm
and swung me off course, her expression was certainly less composed than I'd ever imagined it could be. She still looked like a
nymph, but a determined nymph. "Hurry!" she repeated, tugging
at my sleeve. Instead, I pulled back. Sergeant Boddy was bad
enough, but who knew what Angelica had in mind? "They're
watching your car!" she said breathlessly as we half-ran down one
aisle, skidded to the right and made off speedily along another. I
held my precious bundle firmly to my bosom as we went. Footsteps
behind us made it clear that Melanie was still tagging along. Then
we were diving through a door marked with a dingy FIRE EXIT
sign and out onto a cinder-covered parking area at one side of the
building.

"Wait! Wait! I'm coming." The urgent voice had a British accent. *Oh, God, Cave*, I thought, and ran faster. But it wasn't
Cave. It was Brother Martin, and Melanie's enormous brown dog
was galloping right along with him. Cave was around, though. As
we hurried across the parking lot, I caught a glimpse of him
crouching behind a car near our own.

"Quick!" Angelica said, "get in!" All five of us arrived simultaneously at a car parked by itself at the edge of the lot. What a car

for an anonymous getaway! Angelica's wheels consisted of a fire-engine red Alfa-Romeo sedan, visible at five miles on a foggy night. But there was no time to wish for something sober, like a gray Toyota. Nobody had followed us out of the side exit, but once our car started it could only be a matter of seconds before Boddy and Cave came after us. So I asked no dumb questions about where we were going or why. And as Angelica slipped behind the wheel and got the Alfa started, I jackknifed into the back seat, sharing it on far from equal terms with a breathless Melanie and a grinning, tail-swishing Fig Newton.

The Alfa's wheels spun wildly for a second, then caught, and we came around the corner of the building hell-bent for election and the exit from the parking lot.

"Go right! Go right!" yelled Brother Martin. Angelica set her beautiful mouth, stamped on the brake and twitched the wheel, and the car whipped obediently into a skid that headed us to the right on the hardtop road.

"Newton!" shrilled Melanie. "Behave!" The dog's waving tail partly obscured the rear window, but not enough so I couldn't glimpse what was happening behind us in the parking lot. It would have been funny if it hadn't also been terrifying.

As we slid onto the highway, Boddy and Cave came sprinting out of Ezekiel's main entrance. They paused for a split second, gesticulating furiously like Keystone Cops. Then they ran in the direction of their own car.

My jaw dropped.

From somewhere, they'd commandeered the only car in the world more conspicuous than our own. It was a square-bodied, jet-black Rolls Royce, formal and shiny and as big as a house. The sunlight glittered on its two sets of huge round headlights, on its chrome and on the auto-club emblems affixed to its front grille. I gaped as the enormous thing trundled in reverse out of its parking space and, as we ourselves began to gather speed, rolled magisterially forward after us. It was like being pursued by the entire British Empire.

"Don't look now," I said to Angelica.

"I know," she said impatiently. She stepped on the accelerator.

A DO NOT PASS sign flashed by on the right. Angelica swung the Alfa into the left lane, tapped her horn twice and zipped past a pickup with a pair of dice dangling from its rear-view mirror.

She got us back into the right lane at least three seconds before the gravel truck thundered by on the left.

To this day, I don't know how Boddy or Cave, whichever one was driving the Rolls, got it around the pickup and past the gravel truck. All I heard was the baying of the big truck's diesel horn. But as our car came around a curve to the left and into a long straightaway, there about a quarter-mile behind was the Rolls. We were doing about 70, and for the moment we were holding our own. But the straightaway was taking us steadily uphill. You didn't have to be an automotive engineer to know what would happen in an uphill race between a four-cylinder Alfa compact and a Rolls-Royce. Unless we did something, that is.

"Angelica . . ." I began.

"Do be quiet," she snapped. Then: "Does anybody know where this road goes?"

"I do, as a matter of fact," said Brother Martin.

"Is there any place to turn off?" Angelica demanded. While I watched through the rear window, the Rolls was getting larger and larger.

"Up ahead," Brother Martin said.

"Yes, of course," said Angelica with a God-give-me-patience undertone in her voice, "but could you please tell me where?"

"It's only paved for a little bit of the way," Brother Martin said practically.

"All right, but where?" said Angelica.

"*There,*" Brother Martin said suddenly, pointing.

There was a screech and a smell of rubber as Angelica hit the brakes and our tires bit into the pavement. We barely made it. I won't swear that our two right wheels stayed on the road as we swerved into that insane left turn. It took us off the main highway and onto a narrow, winding two-laner that twisted wickedly uphill past a house or two and into deep woods.

"Jolly good!" exclaimed Brother Martin admiringly. Fig Newton had lost his balance when we turned and landed sprawling in my

140

lap. But he was as enthusiastic as Brother Martin and seized the chance to lick my face with gusto. Melanie, too, seemed unperturbed. I was the only one who was terrified.

The hardtop surface ended abruptly, and we were speeding noisily over a blend of gravel and dirt. For an unpaved road, it wasn't a bad road at all. But the people who'd put it in had never meant for it to be driven at 60 miles an hour.

"Look out!" I shouted. The Alfa jumped crazily as Angelica braked it and then jammed her elegant foot right back on the gas. The two deer I'd spotted in the road not fifty yards ahead bounded off harmlessly into the woods on our right. Sweating, I sank back into my seat.

"You mustn't startle a driver that way," Brother Martin said reprovingly. But I wasn't listening. Over the noise we were making, and there was plenty of it, I thought I heard another sound. I twisted around to look again out of the rear window. The road behind us was empty, but I could only see for a couple of hundred yards.

Then I heard it again. The sound of a loud car horn.

"You know," I said, "I think we're still being followed."

"Of course," said Angelica. "They won't give up. Not yet." She stopped talking to concentrate on the road, which was curving sharply back and forth across the hillside like a playful snake.

"Do you still know where we're going?" I asked Brother Martin. He was clinging with his right hand to the safety grip some prescient Italian had engineered into the top of the Alfa's doorframe.

"Certainly I do," he called back, his teeth gleaming through his beard in an elated smile. "We're going south. In about nine miles this road crosses another one, and that one leads straight down to the Recollects. Actually, we're on our way home."

The road in front of us dipped suddenly. Angelica slowed in time, but I could hear our muffler scrape on the gravel as we splashed through a stream that seemed to have escaped its culvert. As we picked up speed again, Brother Martin yelled something.

"What?" I said.

"It's been a wet summer, hasn't it?"

Good God, the English.

"Tell me something," I said. "Is the road as bad as this the whole way?"

"Oh, no," Brother Martin said cheerfully. "It gets quite a bit worse."

All of the twisting and turning had been to our advantage. I'd been peering back through the rear window for a glimpse of our pursuers, but they still hadn't appeared, and I was feeling better.

"See that old stump?" Brother Martin said as one flicked past us. "That's about the halfway mark."

"Good," I said. But as we spun up out of a hollow and along the edge of a pasture, I heard the horn again. Then, through the dust we were spraying, I caught sight of the Rolls. It was weirdly incongruous in this pastoral setting, but oddly chilling as well. And it was catching up in a hurry.

"The forces of evil are gaining on us," I said.

"Oh, no," said Brother Martin seriously, "those poor men aren't evil. At least, we can't say they are. We can't even assume they're in a state of sin. *Ow!*"

With punishing force, the Alfa hit a bump. We all lurched skyward, but Angelica clung to the wheel, and kept her foot on the accelerator. Rocking on our springs but still game, we kept on going at speed.

"No, no," Brother Martin repeated with inhuman placidity. "The most we are entitled to surmise is that either Covetousness or Envy, or possibly both—oh, I say, *isn't* this fun?"

We'd slammed into another vicious thank-you-ma'am. This time, to my horror, all four wheels left the ground. We were airborne! Transfixed, I stared at the others. Seconds seemed to pass. When we finally jolted down, Fig Newton uttered a thoughtful *Woof*! but nobody else said a word. I'd have to take that one up with Brother Martin, some nice evening when we were all sitting around discussing theology. Tell me, Brother, why don't people react more strongly than dogs do when their lives are in imminent danger. . . .

From behind us came the sudden roar of a huge engine, followed by a heavy thump. I shuddered. The Rolls, too, had taken wing. And landed.

We ourselves were zipping smoothly along, although the road was starting to slope rather steeply downhill. I stole another look out of the rear window. The Rolls was still in sight, but it wasn't gaining on us. Maybe that last bump had bent one of its axles. Maybe when we reached Brother Martin's turnoff, it would keep on going straight ahead out of our lives.

Suddenly, a crack materialized in the Alfa's windshield. It started in the upper lefthand corner and darted like a lizard crookedly toward the right. I watched it, hypnotized, wondering how far it would travel. Angelica muttered something dreadful in German and pushed the Alfa on faster, as if she were punishing it for its weakness.

"Hey," said Melanie anxiously. She'd seen it, too. "Are they *shooting* at us?"

"No," I said. "They wouldn't do that. If we crashed, the manuscript might be destroyed. Besides, they're too far back and the road is much too bumpy." I thought that the beating we'd been giving the Alfa had set up enough strain to buckle the glass. But I did begin to wonder exactly what Boddy and Cave *would* do if they ever caught us.

"The turn you mentioned, Father . . ." Angelica said.

"It's Brother, not Father," Brother Martin corrected her. "About half a mile ahead on the left, you can't miss it. But it is a bit of a drop."

I twisted around again to peer out of the rear window. "Holy Cow!" I said. The Rolls had come down the hill after us like a chromium-fronted bat out of hell. It was barely seventy-five yards behind, and as I watched I was left in absolutely no doubt about what Boddy and Cave had in mind. A blazer-clad arm emerged from the open window on the passenger's side. The gun it was holding had a long barrel. Even at seventy-five yards, it looked as big as a cannon.

"Get down!" I yelled at Melanie. I grabbed her and Fig Newton in my arms and frantically pulled all three of us down and out of view.

"Hold on!" I heard Angelica cry out over my shout. "When I turn, we're going to slide!"

That's when the right front tire blew.

We never did find out afterward whether Cave's brilliant shooting or natural causes had done the deed, but it didn't matter, the result was the same. The blowout turned Angelica's controlled skid into a nightmarish swoop, slow-motion but irresistible. The Alfa's front end first slid rightward, then to the left. In effect, we made the turn into the side road and just kept on turning, so that when Angelica automatically stepped on the gas she ploughed us head-on into the trees and brush that lined the new road on the left.

Wedged with Melanie and a squirming Fig Newton into the slot behind the front seats, I couldn't see a thing. But I heard a horrendous tearing of metal, a crunch, and the tinkling of glass. For perhaps one second, there was silence. Then the second act of the nightmare was upon us. The Rolls, its brakes locked, its tires screaming, had followed us into the turn. But it was going far too fast—so fast that when I raised my head and saw what was happening, I instinctively closed my eyes. But not soon enough.

The Rolls never made the turn. Instead, it shot into the trees across from us and kept on going, into thin air.

Brother Martin had been right, there was a bit of a drop—about fifty feet. There was another second of sickening silence. Then the sound the Rolls made as it landed.

"Please, Mr. French! I can't breathe!" Poor Melanie. I'd squashed her practically through the floor of the Alfa, and Fig Newton with her.

"Are you okay?" I asked as I eased myself gingerly up onto the rear seat.

"I think so," Melanie said. "Alive, anyway. And so is Newton, *aren't* you, honey-bear." The two of them, the girl and the dog, scrambled up beside me. They were disheveled and shaken up but obviously not badly hurt. I could have shouted with relief.

"Man, can't you help me?" Brother Martin was saying exasperatedly from the front seat. "I'm caught, and I've . . . we've got to get *her* out of here."

Angelica was sitting slumped over the steering-wheel. She was very still. Too still.

144

"I'm coming," I said. I've never felt less like exerting myself. It was an effort just to lean forward and tug on the door handle, and when the door swung obligingly open, it was even more of an effort to make my legs obey me and get me out of the back seat.

The afternoon sun was as pleasantly warm on my back as if nothing had happened. I remember listening with incredulity, as if I had no right to listen, to the song of a cardinal in the nearby pines. A stick cracked, the sound unnaturally loud, beneath my foot. Then the sense of dislocation faded. As Newton came bounding irrepressibly out of the car, with Melanie right behind him, I was fumbling with the handle of Brother Martin's door.

If you have to drive a heavily laden automobile off a road at thirty-five miles an hour, you can do a lot worse than run it smack into a heavy growth of maple saplings and evergreens. The Alfa's front fenders, grille, and bodywork were a crumpled mess. The hood was bent upward like an abstract sculpture, and I hated to think what the radiator and fan assembly looked like. But the springy saplings and pine boughs had acted as a kind of a sling, absorbing the worst of the impact. The frame may have been bent, but the passenger compartment was more or less intact. Miraculously, although a whole network of cracks had branched off the one that had started before the blowout, the windshield hadn't shattered. The glass I'd heard tinkling must have been glass from the headlights.

The doorlock on Brother Martin's side worked readily, but the door would only open an inch or so. Stuck. I set my feet firmly, got as good a grip as I could on the handle with both hands and gave a heave. There was a screech of metal on metal, then a snapping as something gave and then the door, reluctantly, came open the rest of the way.

Brother Martin sprang out, so quickly that I knew he couldn't possibly be seriously injured. "Come on," he said, his face tight. "Hurry."

On the driver's side, the door was jammed against a big boulder. Brother Martin threw himself at it, his hands frantically seeking a purchase, the sweat popping out on his face as he strained to get the thing out of the way. "Hold it," I said.

"You must be mad," he said furiously. "We've got . . . to . . . get . . . her . . . out." Again, he threw his weight into an effort to move the rock.

"I think there's a better way," I said. I certainly hoped so: It looked to me that nothing short of a major earthquake was going to shift that piece of granite. Panting, Brother Martin gave up for the moment and stood looking at me. I hurried around to the passenger's side and leaned in to have a look. Angelica hadn't moved. I couldn't tell whether or not she was breathing, but at least there was no sign of blood.

"What in God's name are you doing?" Brother Martin demanded. Beyond him, Melanie and Newton stood watching.

"Just a *minute,*" I said. The Alfa had a manual gearshift. I grabbed the stick, gave a yank and felt the car go out of gear. "Okay," I said. "Now I think we can push it back far enough to get that door open."

"Ah!" The soil underfoot was slippery and there were leaves and dead branches in the way. But in seconds, Brother Martin had cleared the ground. The two of us braced ourselves and started to push. It was no go until we'd gotten rid of one last interfering pine seedling. Brother Martin literally ripped it out of the ground. For a weedy-looking specimen, he had astonishing strength. Then Melanie lent us a hand. One shove by all three of us set the Alfa moving. Another one freed the front door entirely. "Thank God!"

"Easy! Take it easy!" I cautioned. It took Brother Martin and me to force open the door. But he was the one who reached inside and, delicately as a woman, unclipped Angelica's seatbelt and felt for a pulse.

"Her heart's beating," he announced. "*And* she's breathing."

God, how lucky we'd been.

"Should we be moving her?" asked Melanie, but it was too late. Brother Martin, blushing furiously, had slipped one arm around Angelica's shoulders, the other under her thighs and was lifting her gently clear.

"Quick," he said, "pile up some branches and make a bed." But I didn't think he was in any great hurry to set Angelica down.

We threw some piney stuff on a dry spot. Just as Brother Martin

146

was lowering her, Angelica opened her green eyes, gazed at him briefly and closed them again. Her lips curved in her breathtaking smile. Hastily, I looked around for Melanie. I didn't want her to see what was happening to poor Brother Martin. She was only a kid, after all.

Melanie, seated on the ground with an arm around Newton's furry neck, looked at me expressionlessly. Then, in deliberate parody, she opened her eyes very wide, let them droop shut and smiled sultrily. It was devastating. I think that one moment cured me of Angelica forever. I grinned at Melanie—I couldn't help it—and got a real smile in return.

Brother Martin was still fussing. He'd gone over to where a little rill came bubbling down the hillside, wetted his handkerchief and was bathing Angelica's face.

I cleared my throat. Brother Martin gave me a dirty look.

"I had to fetch her out of there," he said defensively. "The car might have gone up like a bomb. The petrol, you know." I looked at the Alfa. Its bright red paint and battered condition gave it the look of a child's abandoned toy. "Well, it might have," Brother Martin insisted.

Mention of the Alfa suddenly made me remember something. I hurried over to it and reached into the rear passenger compartment. From the elasticized pocket on the rear of the right front seat, I fished the bundle containing the manuscript. I'd stuffed it there when the chase began. Already, it seemed like hours ago.

"Here," I gave the bundle to Melanie. "You and Newton hang on to this for a while. Don't open it, and don't give it to anybody." Melanie nodded. "I'll be back in a couple of minutes."

"Where are you off to?" Brother Martin asked. Angelica's eyes were open, I noticed, and she was looking hungrily at the manuscript cradled in Melanie's arms. Melanie looked innocently back at her.

"The Rolls," I said. "It took a hell of a tumble. The people in it may be dead, for all I know. But maybe they're not. I'd better go down there and see."

Brother Martin looked at Angelica, then at me. He moistened his lips. "Yes," he said, "perhaps you'd better. Only . . . be careful."

147

POLYMATHES: *So I perceive that if I had studied of purpose to make an evil lesson I could not have made a worse than this.*

Morley, A Plaine & Easie
Introduction, p. 261

CHAPTER SEVENTEEN

I felt anything but heroic as I crossed the road, worked my way through the briar-laden undergrowth at its far edge and started down the nasty little hill half-hidden by the tangled brush. My legs were already wobbly from the aftereffects of our own crackup, and I was not anxious to learn what awaited me at the bottom of this slope.

Halfway down, I could make out the shiny black top of the Rolls. The huge car was canted at a silly angle against the base of a huge tree. No Rolls Royce should ever look like that, I thought. It's *lèse-majesté*.

A sudden movement made me jump. A gray squirrel dropped from a low limb onto the roof of the wreck. While I watched, it sat there chattering, then it leaped to the ground and scampered off, frightened by something. I knew what, and I began to sweat with apprehensiveness as the sour bile collected in my throat.

Nothing else moved.

Finally, wearily, I let myself down the last fifteen or twenty feet of slope. I stumbled slowly to within a few feet of the Rolls and willed myself to look right at it. Boddy and Cave hadn't been lucky at all. Their windshield was starred and crazed, and on the driver's side a massive branch had smashed its way right through the glass. I went a step or two closer. It was more than enough.

148

The body in the driver's seat was missing its head, or at least the piece of the head the face was on. But unmistakable amid the shredded foliage, the shiny fragments of windshield and the blood that was soaking into everything, was the natty plaid pattern of the suit the body was wearing.

A thought seized me, and I tittered silently. Sergeant Boddy had become a body in fact as well as in name.

The sweat had dried icy-cold on my forehead. I wanted very badly to get the hell back up the hill and out of this secluded little glade. Then I could go tell someone that there had been an accident, and the people who cruise around in police cars and ambulances could come clean up the mess. That certainly was what should happen.

From where I was standing, I couldn't see the far side of the Rolls at all, and the sun was blinding me. Without going closer, I moved to my left to avoid the glare and tried to peer inside. But it was no good. To find out the one other thing I wanted to know, I was going to have to walk right up to the car and its contents, and of course I didn't want to do it.

A few quick strides took me around the tree the Rolls had run into. Now, I could see that at some point during its downhill slalom its passenger door had been thrown open. But again the bright sunlight made it impossible to see into the interior. I gagged at the thought, but at last I got myself moving and covered the last few feet to the car.

At first, it wasn't so bad. The passenger seat was empty. Its upholstery gave off the familiar, friendly odor of good leather, nothing more. Okay, I told myself, you've seen enough. You don't have to look at anything else. You don't have to look at the part of Boddy's head that's lying on the *floor* of the passenger compartment, at the moustache . . .

I sat down unsteadily on a rock. I knew enough to get my head between my knees and keep it there. Eventually, the dizziness went away and I could think. After a fashion.

All right, I said to myself—I won't swear I wasn't talking out loud—now you know exactly what happened. Boddy's down here. Somewhere up there, you'll find Cave. Or what's left of him.

One message was absolutely clear in my mind. I didn't want to find Cave. I was not going to quarter the hillside in search of the late inspector or his component parts. He or they could lie where they were until the cleanup crew arrived.

After a long time, I sat up. Nothing too terrible happened, so I got to my feet and found I could stay upright. Walking like an elderly gentleman with a touch of the gout, I made a wide circle around the wrecked Rolls and started back up the hill. I made a point of not looking too carefully at the humped shapes that somehow seemed to be everywhere on the uneven ground. Rocks and half-rotted tree limbs, most of them, no doubt. And if they were something else, I didn't need to know.

My feet kept going of their own accord, and I was perfectly happy to be climbing up the nice hill. So it was a bit of a surprise to reach the top and the edge of the road and spot the bright red of the Alfa on the far side.

Angelica was sitting up with Brother Martin's black jacket around her shoulders. Brother Martin himself looked up as I approached. "Good Lord, old boy, was it as bad as that? You look white as a ghost."

"Compared to our friends down there," I said, "I look terrific."

Angelica shivered. "Are they . . . ?"

"Oh, yes," I said. Nobody else said anything. It felt chilly under the trees. Instinctively, we all crowded closer together.

And that's how Inspector Cave found us, in a little circle with Angelica at our center.

He wasn't in very good shape, the Inspector. His blue blazer was torn at one shoulder, and blood from a cut was oozing through and darkening the material. His grey slacks, still neatly creased, were spattered and stained, and his brogues were covered with mud. The man himself was in a similar state of disrepair. His eyes didn't look right, and a couple of times a corner of his mouth twitched with nerves. But the long-barreled pistol he held in his right hand was steady enough.

"Everybody please sit still," Cave said quietly.

"You're not dead, then," I said numbly.

Cave almost laughed. "Near enough," he said, "near enough. Now, then, you know what I'm after. Which of you has it?"

"I do," I said.

"She does," Angelica said simultaneously, pointing at Melanie. Cave's gaze flickered from the one to the other. Melanie didn't say a word. She just hugged the bundle I'd given her a little more tightly.

"All right," Cave said to Melanie, holding out his free hand. Melanie shook her head quickly and looked stubborn, the damned little idiot. Cave's mouth tightened. For the first time, he looked really vicious, and I was afraid of what he might do next.

Fig Newton should have known better. All he did was take advantage of Melanie's distraction to wriggle loose and start over to his new friend with the outstretched hand.

Cave should have known better, too.

Coming from a nation of dog-lovers, he should have known that when a big brown dog wags its tail and romps up to you, it wants to play, not tear you limb from limb. But Cave wasn't at his best that afternoon, so he did the wrong thing. He pulled the trigger.

Fig Newton yelped sharply as his new friend's bullet scored his side. At that, he was lucky. An inch to the left and it would have killed him.

Melanie screamed, not very loudly but loudly enough to startle Cave.

Whereupon Brother Martin, with a terrifying growl, launched himself headlong at the astonished Cave, hit him squarely in the midriff and knocked him to the ground, wounded shoulder first.

It was Cave's turn to scream.

His gun flew from his hand, described an arc in the air, landed at my feet and promptly went off again. I leaped back, but the bullet sailed off harmlessly into the air, so I leaned over and cautiously picked up the weapon.

"Christ! keep him off me," Cave panted.

"It serves you right, you . . . you weasel," Melanie said indig-

151

nantly. Newton had fled back to her side and was frantically licking her hand.

"Okay, Brother, okay," I kept repeating. "Enough." By this time, Brother Martin wasn't really doing anything to Cave except standing over him and making those growling noises of his. But I didn't want him to lose control.

Out of the corner of my eye, I caught a hint of movement. "Put it back, Angelica," I said. I wagged the gun for effect. "That's a good girl."

"Hey!" Melanie said. "Give that back!"

"You heard her," I said. "Give it back." Reluctantly, Angelica handed back the half-unwrapped parcel that held the manuscript.

I wagged the gun again. "Can you walk?" I asked Angelica.

"I'll try," she said bravely. Brother Martin murmured something encouraging. Angelica fetched him a big smile as he helped her to her feet.

"And what about you?" I said to Cave. He was sitting up, but he didn't look good. His face was gray, and I thought he must have lost quite a lot of blood. He shot me a venomous look.

"Don't worry about him," Brother Martin said. "He'll manage. And if he can't, I'll help him."

"No, *thank* you," Cave said. He picked himself slowly up.

"Okay," I said brightly, "let's get going. How far did you say it was, Brother M.?"

"From here? About two miles, I should think."

Angelica groaned. "Oooh! In these shoes? I'll never make it."

"Kick them off and go barefoot," I said. To my surprise, she did exactly that. But then, the alternative would have been to let the manuscript get away sight unseen.

To a stranger, we would have looked like something out of the Thirty Years' War. First went Angelica, still wearing Brother Martin's shabby priest's jacket over her shapely shoulders and carrying her shoes in one hand. Then Melanie, the bundle under one arm and a subdued Fig Newton walking stiffly by her side. Cave came next, with Brother Martin to act as his guard, and I brought up the rear, gun in hand. We stopped often to rest our wounded. It

152

took us the better part of an hour to cover the two miles, and absolutely nothing happened on the way.

"Where have you *been?*" Jackie called to me as we came out of the woods by the monastery entrance. "We were getting *frantic.* Ralph's gone in to get Father Gilmary to call the police."

"I'm ready," I said.

Father Gilmary came hurrying out. "Are you all right, my boy?" he asked Brother Martin. Brother Martin gave Angelica one last longing glance.

"Yes, Father, of course," he said.

"Thank God for it. And the rest of you? This poor fellow looks hurt."

"Here, Father." I took the parcel from Melanie and gave it to the priest. Angelica stopped eyeing Jackie and watched hungrily as the manuscript changed hands. Father Gilmary, stunned, stood there holding it.

"So it's back," he said simply.

"Father, please . . . may I see it? Examine it?" There was no stopping Angelica Lederman, or even slowing her down.

"Why, yes, my dear," Father Gilmary said, taking her in for the first time. "Later." He thrust the bundle into Brother Martin's hands. "Take this inside and put it back where it belongs. We've got to get these people some help."

After that, events began to move faster and faster. Lieutenant Catapana came racing up in his unmarked police special. It made me wince to see anybody drive that fast. There was much squawking over police radios and barking of orders as cruisers, wreckers, and an ambulance were dispatched to the scene of our double disaster.

Then Cave got into the act. "Er . . . Lieutenant," he said to Catapana, who looked up incuriously, "I'm Chief Inspector Richard Cave of the Special Branch, British police." He reached into the inside pocket of his blazer, fumbled around for a second and gave an embarrassed grin. "Must have left my warrant card in the car," he said, patting his other pockets absently as he talked.

"Well, I don't suppose it matters. I'd like to request your assistance in taking these people into custody."

"Which people are those?" Catapana said.

"The priest Gilmary and his associate Martin. They're art smugglers."

"Art smugglers," Catapana repeated.

"Yes," said Cave impatiently, his eyes very bright in his exhausted face. "And they've just locked away the bloody loot. It's worth millions of quid, er, Lieutenant, millions of quid."

Catapana stared at Cave in that emotionless way cops do stare at people. Finally, he shrugged. "The place for you, my friend," he said, "is Merriweather Hospital. We'll get you patched up, then we'll see."

"But—"

"I don't guess that Father here will be going anywhere," Catapana said. "Right, Father?"

"Oh, no," Father Gilmary reassured him. "We're staying right here."

"There you go," Catapana said to Cave.

"But these people—"

"Never mind these people," Catapana said, in a voice suddenly ten degrees chillier. "We're going to want to know what you and your buddy were doing to flip over in a three-ton Rolls Royce on a back-country dirt road. After you've told us what *we* want to know, then maybe we'll help you find out what *you* want to know. *Capeesh?*" After that, even Cave knew better than to try to ring Catapana's bell again. Sometime later, Catapana put him in a police car and had him driven away.

With Cave out of action, I breathed easier. In fact, I stopped paying much attention at all to what was going on. I did say goodbye to Melanie and Fig Newton, and Jackie gave Melanie a big hug and thanked her, something I'd completely forgotten to do. Then Melanie went off in a van from Apple Hollow to take Newton to the vet.

Angelica had glued herself to Father Gilmary. When he went inside, she went inside with him. When he reappeared, she was unobtrusively nearby. I wanted to warn him to watch out for Angelica. I thought that proximity to the manuscript, combined with the wild car chase, might be driving Angelica a little crazy. But I was just too tired to do it. After Catapana had arrived, I'd found a garden chair to drop into, and once I was in it I stayed there.

Then we had to give our statements. I kept mine simple. I told Catapana we'd heard a rumor that the missing manuscript had turned up, had gone to Ezekiel's to check out the story, and had actually found and retrieved the manuscript. I didn't say anything about Brother Simon or Angelica, except that Angelica was a dealer from New York City who was interested in the manuscript and had offered us a ride back to the monastery. The two strangers in their big car had chased us from Ezekiel's and had tried to force us off the road. "They were after the same thing we were," I said, "the manuscript."

"And they nearly killed that girl and her dog," Catapana said. He looked at me skeptically. "Anything in what this Cave says about being a British police officer?" I tried to look knowing.

"Could be," I said. "But I think you ought to talk to Father Gilmary about it. Evidently, these guys followed him all the way from England."

"Yeah, okay," said Catapana, "that's what I'll do, I guess. Well, anyway, you got the thing back."

"Right," I said. He made a few more notes, then looked at me and nodded. "Is that it?" I asked him.

"That's it," he said. "For now, anyway. Why don't you and your friends take off? We know where to find you when we want you."

"Sold," I said. The last I saw of Catapana, he was heading purposefully in Father Gilmary's direction.

Later, I learned that Father Gilmary's bout of phoning and cabling about Cave had not been in vain. After one or two more calls, Chief Inspector Cave had been driven under escort from Merriweather Hospital straight to Kennedy International Airport. There, in the company of two large and unsmiling Englishmen, he had boarded a British Airways jet for London, presumably to face the Special Branch equivalent of a summary court-martial. What happened to him after that, I don't know.

After Catapana had finished with me, Ralph offered me the keys of our rental car. I pushed his hand away. "You drive," I said. "Slowly."

"Alan. Alan!" I opened my eyes. It was late evening. We were stopped at Ninety-sixth Street and West End Avenue, stuck in city traffic, waiting for the light to change. I'd dozed or slept most of the way back to New York. I felt terrible.

"Jackie," I croaked.

"It's okay," she said. "I think we'll go to my place. Aren't you glad I didn't get rid of it?" I was glad. I don't think I could have taken the studio that night.

Gentleman that he sometimes is, Ralph drove us all the way downtown to Jackie's walkup and left us there.

"Now," Jackie said an hour later, "isn't this better?"

"Much better," I said. It was, too. First, Jackie had made me take off my shoes and stretch out on her sofa bed. Then she'd warmed us up some soup—not the stuff that comes out of bright red cans but the real soup you decoct from the veal bones your friend Freddie the butcher has saved for you. And what really did make it better was that, after the soup, Jackie had turned the lights low and had come to lie beside me and take me in her arms.

"Now. Tell me," she said, as if to a child.

So I told her most of it. About climbing down the hill and finding poor Boddy dead and climbing back *up* the hill into a holdup. About Brother Martin's overripe concern for Angelica Lederman and his lion-like bravery in going after Cave and his gun. Telling her calmed me, as she knew it would, so that finally my muscles relaxed and I ran out of words and could just lie there with her in the dark thinking about nothing at all.

Suddenly, Jackie's composure cracked, and she started to cry.

"What's wrong?" I asked her.

"Nothing," she sobbed. "Nothing, really. But do you know what day this is?"

"Why?" I said, wriggling around to take a look at the big calendar hanging on her kitchen door.

"It's November fourth," she said.

"Is that important?" I said, really not understanding.

"It's our *wedding* day," Jackie sniffled, "and you could have gotten killed up on that mountainside."

"Oh," I said. "We didn't make it, did we?"

"No," said Jackie.

"But we will," I said.

"Yes," Jackie said. For a long time, neither of us said anything else.

"Hey," I said.

"What?"

"The least we can do is celebrate."

"Celebrate how?"

"Come here," I said, rolling over and reaching for her. "It's my turn to kiss the bride."

Eliza is the fairest Quene,
That ever trod upon this grene,
Elisaes eyes are blessed starres,
Inducing peace, subduing warres.
      "Fairies Song," from Elizabeth's
         Entertainment at Elvetham (1591)

CHAPTER EIGHTEEN

The collar of my brand-new boiled shirt was just scratchy enough to be a nuisance, but there was nothing I could do about it now. In ten minutes or so, we'd be on stage, and a chafing collar would be the least of my troubles.

It was the Saturday before Christmas.

Outside, the first real snow of the season was falling determinedly. The security guard at the stage entrance had grumbled amiably about the weather and about how impossible it would be for him to get out to his sister's in Brooklyn that night. I was about to grumble back when Jackie had headed me off. "Go on," she'd said to the guard, "I'll bet you'll be out there on a sled with your nieces and nephews tomorrow morning." She'd said it with such zest, and she'd looked so wonderful, with snow in her hair and more snow on the case of her gamba, that despite himself the guard had given her a grin, checked our names quickly, and waved us all past his desk.

The snow hadn't discouraged the audience. Ever since the word had started to spread about Elizabeth's music-book and our concert, we'd been the act to catch that Saturday night. Bookings were so heavy that Father Gilmary and I had taken a gamble and switched us from Alice Tully Hall to Avery Fisher. The gamble had paid off. We were sold out, and as we'd made our way downtown on the subway—on a night like this, forget about cabs—we'd overheard the chatter of groups of people on their way to the box office to try for standing room. It was disconcerting, to hear strangers talking about us and our music *before* we'd given the performance. I'd said something about it to Ralph as we were climbing the stairs from the street level to the elevator. He'd grinned a sour grin. "Um. Like hearing the surgical team discussing your brain while you're waiting outside the operating room."

Now Ralph was sitting in misery on a wooden chair in the corner of the dressing room nearest the john. He had on mittens, his overcoat, and a huge furry hat. Beneath the hat, his face was absolutely bloodless, whiter even than his white tie. As always before a concert, I wondered how Ralph was going to make it to the stage.

To tell the truth, we were all scared. Not because the music was hard. We'd all played works a lot more difficult than anything dear old Queen Bess had written down in that damned book—if she'd actually done the writing, that is. No. What scared us about the music was the clarity, the translucency, of what we were going to be playing. This music is like Mozart, I thought to myself for the thousandth time. Everybody's part, simple or not, is *heard.* Every note counts. Even a tiny mistake looms up like Mount Everest. There's no place to hide.

Apart from this worry, I was the only one of us who had ever played here before. And when I'd played, I'd been buried safely and anonymously in the string section of a big orchestra. Even then, I'd found the place intimidating.

In our contract, we'd provided for one rehearsal on the enormous Avery Fisher stage, just to get used to the feel of the house. It may have been a mistake. Yesterday afternoon, when we'd rehearsed, we'd all been exhausted and not playing well. The sound technicians had gone away somewhere. Without their tender loving care, our piping and plunking and fiddling had echoed shrill and bodiless in the empty auditorium. The experience was so demoralizing that we'd skipped the spaghetti with clam sauce we'd promised ourselves and had gone straight back to the studio for two more hours of work.

159

Not least, of course, was the occasion itself. It was fine to say that the Antiqua Players were a success. So we were, but were we ready for Avery Fisher Hall? Only a tiny handful of groups as specialized as we are ever do make it to that exalted height in music, and let's be honest, we are not the Budapest String Quartet. For us, the top was bound to seem a cold and windy place. If we did well here tonight, then maybe it would get a lot warmer. If we didn't. . . .

I awoke from my daydream of national tours and recording contracts and went into the Green Room next door to find Jackie. She was wearing a new dress, ruby-red velvet, and she looked stunning. She smiled at me, but she didn't say anything. I knew that she, like the rest of us, was feeling the pressure. Even Terry was fidgeting. He was playing the sackbut—a softer version of the trombone—in our opening number, and for the ninth time by actual count he'd taken off and polished the mouthpiece.

Snap!

I whirled around as if a wasp had stung me. It was David. "Aw . . . sugar," he said.

We have a superstition about profanity before a concert. Jackie had started the superstition three years before, by declaring somewhere or other that the male Antiqua Players were collectively the foulest-mouthed group she'd ever met, and that if we didn't change our ways she would wash out all our mouths with soap. Since then, we'd done our best not to Use Language, as my great-aunt would have phrased it.

David was still standing there looking foolish. Dangling from his hand was the broken lace of the shoe he'd been re-tying when disaster had struck.

A handsome youth in a vivid green blazer stuck his head in at the door. The assistant stage manager. "Five minutes," he said and disappeared.

Jackie sighed. From the enormous handbag she always carries with her to performances, she extracted a set of men's black shoelaces. One of them she rolled up and stuck back in the handbag for the next time. The other she handed to David. She did all of this in dead silence, but she nevertheless managed to convey a vast and freezing disdain.

"Okay, okay," David mumbled, threading the new lace into his shoe. "I shouldn't have been messing with my shoelaces. I'm sorry. But you don't have to treat me like I was six years old."

"Don't I?" Jackie said dangerously.

At this point, I decided that the time had come. I slipped into my dressing room and grabbed the small box I'd been hiding under the pile of street clothes on my chair. Then I rejoined the others in the Green Room. Jackie and David were still eyeing each other, ready to bite. Terry was pretending not to notice. When nobody was looking I opened the box and took out what was inside. Then I set it going.

"E-e-ek!" Jackie said. She said it exactly as girls say it in comic strips. Terry dropped the mouthpiece of the sackbut. David, still holding one shoe in his hand, jumped approximately eight inches.

"Oh, God," Ralph moaned despairingly from the doorway, "what has he done now?"

The little plastic pig made a whirring noise as he jumped about on the table. He was a sweet little creature, and he certainly had rhythm. His curly tail spun around like a propeller. But the best and most mysterious thing about him was the green plastic four-leaf clover that hung from his chin and jiggled and wobbled crazily as he did his dance.

Suddenly we were all laughing. First, Jackie collapsed onto a sofa with a fit of the giggles. Then David began hopping dementedly around the room, in flawless imitation of our tiny porker. Even Ralph forgot his nerves and his tummy and began to laugh. Terry was the worst. He actually fell to the floor and rolled around with tears in his eyes. But we were all beside ourselves.

In the midst of this mania, the door opened. It was the assistant manager again, all set to give us the two-minute signal. But he never gave it. Instead, he took one look at the goings-on and hastily closed the door. Jackie, who had calmed down slightly, began to laugh all over again. "His . . . his . . ." she gasped, trying to catch her breath.

161

"His what?" I demanded.

"His jacket," she gulped. "It's the same color green as . . ." she pointed weakly at the pig's four-leaf clover.

"Of course," I said. "They both want to wish us good luck." Everybody thought that was very funny, too.

Eventually, the pig's gyrations slowed and stopped and we could pull ourselves together. We got Terry dusted off and into his tailcoat. Ralph fled into the bathroom, but he stayed there only briefly and came out looking almost normal. Without incident, David put on and tied his shoe. We carefully avoided one another's eyes, just as we avoided looking over at the pig. But the little fellow had done his job. He'd swept away the tension and made us relax in spite of ourselves.

I was last on Jackie's tour of inspection. She tweaked my white tie once and nodded approvingly. "Clown," she said.

"Hold still," I said.

"What for?"

"This." I gave her a swift kiss. "Okay," I said, straightening up, "the order will be Jackie, David, Terry, Ralph, me. David, give Jackie room, she's carrying her fiddle. And let's everybody give her enough time to set it down before we bow.

"Who's got an A?" We tuned up for our opener. We'd have to tune again afterward, but I like to appear on stage and start the program without a lot of preliminary buzzing and humming, and I think the audience likes it, too.

Instruments in hand, we filed out of the dressing room and along the hall. The lad in the green blazer was holding the elevator for us. Silently, it took us down one level, right into the wings. We paused, and I could feel some of the tension creep back into me. No wonder. On the far side of that doorway, the one with the black muslin curtain across it, three thousand of Ralph's surgeons were waiting to slice us to the bone and find out what, if anything, we had inside.

We stood there while a couple of Avery Fisher stagehands held a colloquy about the state of last week's deer hunting in Owego County, it was great, yeah, right, but didja hear what happened to Eddie? The discourse went on and on. I caught Terry's eye and he

162

winked. His forehead was damp with sweat. "Unreal," he mouthed silently, jerking his chin at the two huntsmen. I grinned and nodded, licking my lips to keep them from getting too dry.

At last, one of the Nimrods peered around the edge of the curtain and motioned us ahead. "Let's count first," I whispered. Everybody pressed closer together to hear better. "One and two and three and four *and play.*" With the beat of the first number echoing in our minds like a group mantra, we trooped on stage. It was a long, long hike across those acres of scuffed floor to our places. I could feel my nerves jumping as we all faced blindly into the darkness out front and heard the swell of the polite applause that greeted our opening bow.

Then something peculiar happened.

For orchestra musicians, the pit gets to be like home. At some performance or other, you've probably spotted through your opera glasses the kind of thing I mean. One of the violists will spread her needlework out around her, and even during a string-and-woodwind *tutti* the old hands in the brass section will be keeping their pinochle games going strong. But out on the recital stage, the whole environment is so unhomelike, so unfamiliar, that it's conducive to weird imaginings. That night at Fisher Hall, I think I was momentarily off my trolley. *What the hell are you doing up here in those funny clothes?* a voice asked me as I took my seat. *Beats me,* I answered dreamily, and I think I would have sat there forever, waiting to find out. But then I glanced down at my music stand, and there, lit up by the little lamp, was the one thing in my sensory universe that wasn't disorienting: the music; the familiar, dog-eared, finger-marked parts and scores I'd been living with for weeks on end. The one look was enough to clear my head. *Oh. Okay. Time to go to work.*

Ralph and Terry were looking at me strangely. I didn't blame them a bit, but there was no time even to shrug them an apology for my lapse of attention. I put the capped reed of the krummhorn to my lips and gave them the upbeat.

Our opening trio was the kind of Tudor court music a young princess might well have heard, remembered, and even copied into her music-book, much as a girl today might buy and keep the sheet music of a favorite show tune. The piece had probably been written for brass, and in brass it would have made a nice, rousing introduction to the evening. James Weede and his Consorte would have done it that way. But I'd wanted to start with something subtler, something to suggest the melancholy that entangles with the brightness in Elizabethan music. So I'd gambled. I'd scored the trio for a peculiar combination: sackbut, cornetto, and krummhorn.

Ralph had spent weeks struggling with the cornetto. It's got a mouthpiece like a trumpet, so you need a lip to play it, and a lip can be painful to acquire. At first, Ralph had hated the cornetto. "Ugh. Like a rooster with a speech impediment." But he'd gotten better and better, and then he'd begun to like it—as much as Ralph can ever like any instrument that's not a harpsichord.

Halfway through the second strain, I sensed that the audience was interested. Our subdued beginning may have caught people a little off balance, but the house had quieted down to catch our quiet sound. Now that I'd stopped behaving so oddly, Terry and Ralph had relaxed. We were just moving along and letting the music play itself. My biggest concern was to keep enough air going into my krummhorn. Do that, and you get a wonderful sound that's a cross between a cruising honeybee and a giant kazoo. Forget for a moment, and your krummhorn sounds more like a leaky inner tube.

We ended to a scattering of applause. While the latecomers wriggled their way to their seats, we got ourselves ready for the next number. My eyes were adjusting to the lights, and through the gloom out front I could see that the place was packed. The realization did things to my adrenals. We quickly checked our tuning, got set on the beat, and went right into the music.

Our second offering was exactly what this audience wanted: bright, brisk tunes and plenty to watch on stage as well as plenty to hear. I'd grouped three dance pieces into a little suite, and I'd arranged the music for treble viol, two recorders, lute, and gamba, so that all five of us were playing. Ah, Avery Fisher! Since they rebuilt it, the acoustics have been remarkable. Our ensemble sound was delectable, though I say so myself. (The fact that the

164

sound technicians were on the job *may* have made a difference.) Also, we were passing the melody from player to player on repeats, so that everybody was getting in some good licks. This time, the applause when we ended was a lot stronger.

Now for our first solo.

Ralph put aside his recorder, stood up and walked over to his harpsichord. "He looks tired," I whispered to David. David, who never looks tired, shrugged unsympathetically, but I felt a twinge of anxiety as Ralph flipped his tails back over the bench and settled himself to play.

His solo was one of the real finds in the manuscript, a set of variations on a piece by Thomas Tallis called "O Ye Tender Babes." The Tallis theme was known from several sources, but not the variations. They were big music. Some of them were full of blocky chords and complex inner harmony. Some were tricked out with strings of sixteenth notes that ran up and down the keyboard and, without the tiny pauses that marked the phrasing, went nowhere.

I don't know how well Queen Elizabeth would have done, but Ralph Mitchell knocked those tender babes right out of the ballpark. He very wisely moved lightly through the chordal variations. The purists might have panned him for not bringing out the inner voices enough—they always pan keyboard players for that—but I say that harpsichord sound decays too fast, at least under concert conditions, and that what you need for the inner voices is a chamber organ. But who cares? Ralph didn't happen to be playing a chamber organ that evening.

The big moment came in the fancywork variations. Tallis put in three of these, one right after the other. In the first, the left hand carries the tune in the bass while the right hand uncoils the strands of sixteenth notes. In the second, the right hand has the theme and the left hand does the uncoiling. In the third, both hands dart all over the place like mice.

Ralph started the first variation at so fast a tempo that I found myself pushing back in my seat and muttering, *Put on the brakes, you damn fool, you'll spoil everything.* But his fingers never faltered, and he spun the first variation to a close and shot into the second at a speed just as fast or even a shade faster. I held my breath. Sure enough, in the third variation Ralph made those fingers move so fast they blurred. It was virtuoso stuff. Yet he never sounded forced, he did let his phrases breathe, and he didn't seem to be pushing into the keys, a heinous vice of which many harpsichordists, including Ralph, are only too ready to accuse other harpsichordists.

The third variation ends in a burst of digital fireworks and a fat six-part chord. Ralph arpeggiated the chord and made it lead into the final variation, which is a slow, slightly elaborated reprise of the theme. Only then did I let out my breath. At last, Ralph tucked the last tender babe to sleep and sat quietly at the keyboard. He was expecting a roar of applause, the artful ham, and he got it, but he deserved everything they gave him and more.

An *ottavino* is a tiny harpsichord on which each note is pitched an octave higher than its key on the keyboard. This gives it an entertaining nasal sound that was perfect for the next item on our menu, a fluffy little three-part Italian canzonetta. We thought it would be just the thing to follow the Tallis, and once again a programming gamble paid off. Ralph switched to the ottavino, and he and David on lute tossed the tune back and forth, plucked string answering plucked string, while Jackie carried the bass line. Then Terry and I joined in on tenor recorders, which sounded cheerful and shifted the focus nicely from a soloist back to the whole group.

As we finished the final strain, I allowed myself a small smile of pleasure. Everything was going smoothly, everybody was playing well. And now, to round out the first half of the performance, Alan French was going to enchant the audience with a display of his brilliance on the wooden flute.

Midway through Elizabeth's manuscript, there appeared a sequence of three anonymous song tunes. One of them sounded vaguely like a piece called "Pawles Wharfe," by the keyboard composer Giles Farnaby. The others were completely unfamiliar, but all three were charming, and ideal for flute. Jackie and David were going to supply the accompaniment, and I would warble away to my heart's content. I was looking forward to it. While the crowd was still clapping for the canzonetta, I reached out to set up the music.

It wasn't there.

A cold sweat began to stand out on my forehead. Oh, Christ, where is it? It's in a white folder, a dirty white folder, all taped and stapled in place so I wouldn't have to worry about any awkward page turns. *It must be here. Hunt for it. Be methodical.* I was methodical. I searched carefully through the sheaf of parts and scores in front of me. None of the others was missing, or even out of sequence. Only this one. And I needed it. On it, I'd penciled in every breath-mark, every phrase, every retard, every repeat sign, for nearly six straight minutes of solo flute. Now it was gone. What on earth was I going to do?

The applause was dying down. In a few seconds, I should be ready, flute in hand.

The hell of it was, nobody *else* had the music, either. Jackie was playing from a bass part, not from a complete score that included my part. David's music was written out in lute tablature, which in no way resembles ordinary staff notation.

It was absurd. It was nightmarish.

To be sure, I could rise to my feet and say jovially to the audience: "Pardon me, ladies and gentlemen, I seem to have left my music for the next piece back in the locker room. Just take a break for a few minutes, won't you, while I run back and get it?" Now, that would certainly establish our reputation. Just like that ball player, I forget his name, who scooped up a fumble and ran fifty yards for a touchdown—against his own team. The reviewers might forgive us, but first they'd turn us into a bumbling bunch of amateurs. Besides . . . what if the music wasn't even in the dressing room when I got there? What if I'd left it back in the studio?

The memory flashed through my mind of a tenor in Bologna who had mangled his big aria. The Bolognese take their opera seriously. They'd chased the tenor off the stage, out into the street and through the town to the train station, where they'd put him on the next outbound express and told him never to come back.

I had two choices. Either I could skip my solo or else I could try it from memory.

Oh, God.

God didn't answer. So, fighting back panic, I picked up my flute with fingers that were already slippery and trembling. Could I do it? I wasn't even sure I remembered the first note. But Jackie and David were waiting expectantly, and I remember thinking that it wasn't fair to keep them waiting all evening. What the hell, I said to myself with false bravado, and gave them the upbeat.

My fingers found the first note for me, and then the first phrase, and I knew at once what I'd have to do if I were going to get myself through this horror. *The best way to remember is to forget.* I was going to have to focus on anything and everything else *except* the flow of the music, and trust my fingers and the back part of my brain to find their way through. They could do it, I told myself cheerily. They'd played these little pieces dozens of times, maybe hundreds of times, and this is just one more of those times.

It seemed to be working. We were nearing the end of the first strain of the first song. The old fingers were dancing up and down on the holes of the flute as automatically as if they were powered by transistorized circuits. I even found myself listening with pleasure to the nuances of David's lute as he filled in the harmony. Now, was this the one where we'd agreed to skip the repeat . . . ?

Stop *thinking*. Now, breathe. Listen to David and Jackie. Are they repeating? Yes, they are, so just go with them.

It was exactly like driving through heavy fog. At any instant, your eyes and ears tell you that everything is normal. The wipers are beating reassuringly back and forth, the radio is still dishing out familiar pop, the car is still on the road. In front of you and behind you is blank whiteness, but if you don't think about it you won't freeze and jam the wheel to one side or the other.

It *was* working. We were halfway through now, and I hadn't made a single serious mistake. The notes were flowing easily. I was a little tired, though, and it might be a good idea just to edge my mind into those tiny ornaments I'd worked into the second repeat.

It was a lousy idea.

Suddenly, I was lost.

As before, I was listening to the smooth coherence of David's lute and Jackie's gamba. It sounded lovely. But I had no idea where my own part fitted or what I was supposed to do next. The fog had closed in, the car was swerving to one side. . . .

Calm down. Wait for the end of the bar. The best way to remember is to just let your fingers do the walking, they know their way around in this tune even if you don't, so keep *calm* and give them a chance.

Listen. Breathe. *Play.* And there I was, back into the music.

Across from me, Jackie cocked her head and gave me a little moue of relief. David stopped moving his shoulders to feed me the beat and began to concentrate once again on his fingerwork. The car was back on the road. I even managed to put together some fresh ornamentation, improvised on the spot in the best Renaissance tradition, to make up for what I'd skipped. Then we were into the last strain of the last song, headed toward the close and my heart began to race because I was actually going to make it all the way through this impossible, terrifying, *stupid* situation.

The final cadence. Remember to vibrate slowly. Slowly. NOW. With a little waggle of the flute, I cut off the sound and it was over.

I lowered the flute and stood there inanely. When the applause began, I almost forgot to bow. They weren't giving me the ovation they'd given Ralph. Even as I trembled with relief that my six-minute ordeal was over, I was unhappy about that. So much for Alan French's modesty as an artist.

My knees were so unsteady that when I finally did take a bow, I nearly fell over, which would have served me right. But I recovered my balance and made the proper gracious gestures, first to Jackie and David, then to all four of the others. They arose, acknowledged the applause, sat down, arose again. At long last, the clapping died away, the house lights came on, and I could totter offstage.

One of the lighting technicians winked as we passed him in the wings. He held up a hand with the thumb and middle finger crooked in an "O" to mean an okay performance. Nice guy. Too bad he wasn't writing the review in the *Times.*

Green Blazer had the elevator waiting.

"What the hell . . . ?" Terry asked me when we were all inside.

"Not here," I said. "Upstairs. Ralph, I hate you. You stole the first act. You were sensational."

"Well, I must admit I *am* pleased," Ralph said. He spoke seriously, but his eyes were sparkling and every few seconds an enormous grin lit up his face. His delight was so irresistible that it chased all my envy away. I grabbed him, wrapped my arms around him in a hug and kissed him on both cheeks.

"Aha!" said Terry. "Like a *goombah*!" And he ruffled Ralph's hair and gave him a smacking kiss right on the mouth. The elevator lurched to a stop, but Green Blazer had to wait in the open door, goggle-eyed, while Jackie and David took their turns hugging and kissing our star. Poor Green Blazer. First the pig, then this. I'm sure he believes to this day that we're totally unhinged.

The pig was just where we'd left him, on the table in the Green Room. And right next to him was a dirty white folder, smudged and dog-eared. The minute I saw it, I remembered. I'd pulled it out to mark a new phrasing I'd decided to use, and I'd never put it back with the rest of my music.

"There you are, you little son of a bitch," I said, dropping exhausted into a chair.

"There *who* are?" Terry asked.

"My music," I told him. "I left it up here."

"You mean, you didn't have it downstairs?" said Jackie. I shook my head.

"Somebody get me a Coke," I said, "I'm really beat."

"Here," Terry said. I sucked in sugar, caramel, caffeine, and phosphoric acid, whatever that is, and started to revive.

Terry shook his head slowly. "You're too much. Know what I mean? You played that thing from your head. In Lincoln Center. Man, you're out of your gourd."

"You could be right," I said. "It was a crazy thing to do."

"Is that why you were all over the place in that third piece?" David asked.

"That's why," I said.

"Thank God," he said. "I thought it was me."

"Listen," I said. "You guys all did beautifully. I'm the one this time. I came so close to screwing us up, I get gooseflesh just think-

170

ing about it. Next half, before anything happens, I'm going to sit there on stage and go through my music. If anything isn't there that should be, I'm going to get up and go home."

"Ralph, that was mighty nice work. Jackie, Terry, David, your turns are coming up." I leaned back in my chair and relaxed.

"What's this?" asked Jackie. "No more pearls of wisdom from the maestro?"

"Not a one," I said. Then, "Oh, yes. We do two encores, then if they still want more we repeat "Eliza." Now, let me snooze."

Terry and David whiled away the intermission by practicing one of their openings. Ralph stayed on his feet, moving restlessly between dressing room and Green Room, picking out a few notes on the practice piano, then wandering off somewhere else.

"What are you doing, Jackie?" I called to her. I was too lazy to turn around and find out.

"Finger exercises."

"Oh." I settled myself more comfortably and closed my eyes. The room was filled with the familiar sounds of my companions in crime at their warmups. For the moment, the stage and all of those people out in front seemed far, far away. That was soothing. In fact, delicious. I couldn't have fallen all the way asleep. But I must admit that when Green Blazer popped in to announce the three-minute signal, I would have been happy to go on sitting in my chair.

A little cold water splashed on the face took care of that.

"Alan, are you all right?" Jackie looked at me dubiously as we walked together to the elevator.

"Yes, absolutely," I said, and I meant it. The few minutes of rest had been a godsend. My nerves had stopped quivering. I was eager to see what we would do in the second half.

Jackie gave her hair a quick once-over in the mirror across from the stage doorway. Then she said, "My turn," and leaned over to give me a kiss; and we all paraded out to our places to the pleasant sound of applause.

I felt even better after my first really complicated bit of music, a two-part dance I played on the treble viol to Terry's treble recorder. It was quick and tricky, but we carried it off without a hitch. "Aw *right!*" Terry muttered to me as we took our bows.

Even so, without Jackie the second part of the program might have been an anticlimax.

The great composer William Byrd had written a song for voice and viols called "Where Phoebus Us'd To Dwell." After the execution of Mary Queen of Scots, one of Mary's sympathizers wrote strange new words to Byrd's exquisite music, about "the noble famous Queen/Who lost her head of late." A set of divisions, or variations, on Byrd's song had found its way into Elizabeth's manuscript. Was it a sign of one queen's grief over the fate of another?

The song itself and the final variation I had scored for viols and recorders. But the eight long variations at the heart of the piece sounded to me like Byrd's own work, and they could have been composed only for solo gamba.

After the first few bars, I stopped listening to Jackie with a professional's ear. I knew she had the skills to solve the technical problems of the music. I knew from rehearsals that she'd play the Byrd with marvelous lightness and delicacy, which made brilliant sense because too often performers give Byrd solemn, heavyhanded treatment. And as those opening measures unfolded, I knew one other thing. The self-assurance that comes so slowly to the musician had come at last to Jackie. Her authority over the music was astounding. And it communicated itself, so that as she played her rapport with her audience grew stronger and stronger. Under my eyes, a gifted instrumentalist had ripened into a great instrumentalist, the kind who packs concert halls and produces magic. Jackie Craine had arrived.

After the Byrd, we played "Eliza's Galiardo."

First I stood up and gave my little spiel about the possibility that Queen Elizabeth herself, while still a young princess, had not only copied but composed the music. The audience loved that, and ate up the galiardo itself. We did do two encores, and we did have to play Eliza again before the crowd would let us go. It was lots of fun. But there was no doubt in anybody's mind that during that

last hour the memorable music had flowed out of Jackie's viola da
gamba.

We got ourselves offstage and headed for the elevator, too
keyed up to talk much, but all of us wearing smiles and needing to
touch each other. I stopped Jackie in the hallway outside our
dressing room. I wanted to kiss her. I wanted to say something, to
do something that would express the unruly mixture of feelings—
love, envy, respect, sadness—churning away inside me. But all I
could do was stare, and all she could do was stare back. Finally, I
said the first thing that came into my head: "Gee. Can I be you?"
It was a strange thing to say. I said it jokingly, and yet I really
meant it.

Jackie looked at me lovingly. "Yes," she said. "But not all the
time." While I was digesting that, she laughed lightly and stepped
closer. We gave each other a quick squeeze—it's not easy to hug a
girl who's carrying a large stringed instrument and its bow in one
hand—and went in to find the others.

You never know who's going to show up to see you backstage
after a concert, or whether or not anybody's going to be there at
all. Tonight, lack of company clearly wasn't going to be the problem. "Brace yourselves, my dears," Ralph said as we walked in,
"the loud world awaits us." We could indeed hear the loud world
on the far side of the Green Room door.

"Yum, champagne!" said Jackie. Sure enough, there on the
table next to the pig was a bottle of Mumm's Cordon Something
in a plastic ice bucket.

"Who sent us this?" I wondered out loud, exercising my thumbs
on the cork.

"I did." It was Mickey Weintraub, our lawyer, resplendent in
silk and mohair.

"Oh, my God, what's wrong?" Mickey never, never shows up at
classical music performances, so I assumed automatically that we'd
been caught doing something dreadful. But Mickey waved his
cigar to establish our total innocence and brushed aside my thanks
for the wine.

"Just here to see the show, kid. And in case anything interesting happens. Enjoy the fizz. No, don't pour me any. Gives me heartburn." The rest of us each had a paper cup of champagne, and we voted a cup apiece to Green Blazer and to the young friend of Ralph's who'd turned his pages for him and had collected our instruments and music for us after we'd left the stage.

By this time, the buzz of voices outside had become more like a dull roar. So we tidied ourselves up a bit, opened the door and peeked out. It was unbelievable, almost like a rush-hour subway. And an astonishing thing happened. Like gentlemen, the four male Antiqua Players waited for Jackie to go through the door. And as she did, the whole crowded Green Room broke briefly into applause. It was a real tribute. Jackie blushed rosy red, but she held her head high and smiled her thanks, and looked absolutely smashing. She turned to say something to me, but the gabble of voices drowned her out and then a mob of well-wishers swept us apart.

For half an hour or more, people were rushing up to shake hands, mumble or shout congratulations and tell me things— about the way we'd played, about the manuscript, about Queen Elizabeth, about anything. Two people asked me for jobs with the Antiqua Players. Neither of them had pencil or paper to write down their names. One lady, in wall-to-wall mink, wanted advice on setting up an early music group of her own. Its purpose, I gathered, was to perform at meetings of her bridge group. A short, perspiring man introduced himself as the cultural affairs editor of a financial weekly, asked for and got my home phone and then asked for Jackie's. When I shook my head, he grinned a reporter's knowing grin. "So that's it," he said. "Can't say I blame you. But what about if I ask her myself?" That was fine with me, I lied, and he laughed and squeezed my arm and set off through the press of people in search of Jackie.

Finally, the crowd began to thin out. I was thinking of ducking back into the dressing room to take another sip of champagne and rest my weary bones. But a gathering across the room made me do a double take, and I decided to stay around for a while longer.

There was Father Gilmary, his handsome profile in relief against

174

the white wall, his face creased in a smile. I certainly expected to see him here, and to see nearby the awkward figure of Brother Martin. But the two other people with them I did not expect to see. One was Angelica Lederman. She had her back to me, and if her turquoise brocade dress was cut as low in front as it was in back, then Brother Martin was undoubtedly in serious trouble, along with most other males in the vicinity. Come to think of it, Brother Martin did have on a hungry, Augustinian look. Even so, it was the fourth member of the crew who made me whistle silently to myself. I'd have expected Tarleton Morlock to be at the concert: We were the thing to do in New York that evening. But what was Morlock doing in the company of the other three?

It didn't take long to find out. Father Gilmary caught sight of me and immediately waved me over. "Why, if it isn't the very man himself!" he called gaily. "I've been looking for you to congratulate you! You were magnificent, and especially Miss Craine! And Mitchell! Marvelous, all of you."

I murmured my thanks, eyeing the others meanwhile as if we were all perfect strangers. But Father Gilmary was having none of my well-bred reticence. He wanted us all to be friends.

"Of course, you and Miss Lederman know each other," he said. "She's been *so* helpful. And if I'm not mistaken, you've met Mr. Morlock as well." Morlock's lantern-jawed face was expressionless for a moment, then he grinned his most charming, most insolent grin.

"Oh, yes," he said. "On several occasions. I even gave him lunch. The last time, he was furious because I was burglarizing his little nest. Weren't you?"

I gave him grin for grin. "Well, it wasn't the burglary so much," I said. "It was more the damage you were trying to do to my hands. That I thought was a bit . . . sadistic. What do you think, Father?" I had the satisfaction of seeing Morlock's self-assurance fade slightly, but only slightly.

"Come, come, we can't have this," said Father Gilmary reprovingly. "Not when there's so much to celebrate."

"Like what?" I asked.

175

"Your concert, for one thing," Father Gilmary said. "That and. . . ."

"Oh, do tell him," said Angelica Lederman with a melting, mocking smile.

"It's certainly no secret," said Father Gilmary. "At least, it won't be by morning. But the fact is, it's sold."

"Sold," I said stupidly. "You mean the manuscript."

"Yes, absolutely. Through Miss Lederman."

"But. . . ."

"You thought it was going to auction."

"At Christie's."

"It can be withdrawn. Tarleton's arranging it." Tarleton? Light was beginning to dawn.

"You've sold it to Morlock," I said.

"Exactly. And at a marvelous price."

"How much?" I asked.

"None of your goddam business," said Morlock.

"Oh, tell him," said Angelica again.

"Yes, certainly," said Father Gilmary, "French has every right to know. We're receiving two million seven hundred thousand dollars."

"Two million seven," I said. Father Gilmary nodded. "Not bad. He offered me six or seven thousand for it. *Before* he tried to steal it."

"Is that true, Morlock?" Father Gilmary asked.

"Would you believe a word he says?" Morlock said, glaring at me.

Two million seven. I was looking at Father Gilmary, but I was seeing other things. Like Brother Simon's smirking face, and the way the woman Selma had stood smiling and rocking back and forth and hating me at Ezekiel's, and Sergeant Boddy's torn face and bloody moustache on the floor of the wrecked Rolls Royce. *Where did they get the Rolls?* I wondered suddenly, knowing that it didn't matter, and that in any case I'd never find out.

I turned to Angelica. "Were you and Morlock in the deal from the start?" I asked her. Angelica didn't answer directly. She simply smiled and moved her body slightly inside her dress, making me aware of her and her power. You don't need to know that, she was saying wordlessly. Anywhere, any time, I can get my share of whatever there is to gain.

Father Gilmary's joviality had faded a little. Perhaps he was guessing what was going on in my mind, that the people he was doing business with were a poor lot to succeed to the ownership of a great queen's heirloom.

The Green Room was almost empty now.

"Merry Christmas, Father," I said. "A merry, merry Christmas to you."

The ornamentation alters the melody, rhythm, and harmony of the music. Its study is, therefore, indispensable.

Arnold Dolmetsch, The Interpretation
of the Music of the XVII & XVIII
Centuries (1916), p. 88

CHAPTER NINETEEN

The affair of the sale was a nine days' wonder. Christie's, as you might expect, made a terrible fuss. First they threatened to sue everybody and then they announced that they were pleased to be rid of the manuscript, since it was stolen, smuggled, forged, and not by Queen Elizabeth anyway. Nobody paid any attention. *The New York Times* ran a long feature on the manuscript. They quoted many experts, but chiefly Tarleton Morlock, on the issue of authenticity. They rubbed their hands on the issue of price, but decried that England had once again lost a national treasure to a rich, greedy overseas buyer.

The owner of Ezekiel's made the eleven o'clock news. "If I'd-a known it was that valuable," he declared, "I'd-a definitely handled it different." The publicity was so good for him that he opened his doors in the dead of winter and did a land-office business.

We haven't done too badly ourselves. Father Gilmary, I must say, was generous to us. Before he and Brother Martin flew back to England with their loot, he waived in our favor the rights of the Oratorians of St. Loy to any concert proceeds. The concert grossed over sixty thousand dollars. After expenses, including the rent for Avery Fisher Hall, the programs, the tickets, the publicity fliers, and the incidentals, and after paying Mickey Weintraub and replenishing our own personal bank accounts, we netted nearly twenty thousand dollars. We've signed a contract for a performing edition of the music. A couple of record companies are nosing around, but Mickey says it's a few weeks too soon. "Wait," he says, "and first get yourselves a manager."

We haven't done that yet. But the week after the concert, *Newsweek* ran a review of us. It began: "Led by a dazzling brunette" and ended "more of Jackie Craine's, and their, elegant musicianship," and Ivor Rhys came to see Jackie.

Ivor Rhys's real name can't possibly be Ivor Rhys. But Rhys is the top gun at Victor Associates and quite possibly the best classical manager in the music business. He made Jackie no promises. He simply said in his soft voice that he had been at our concert, was impressed with Jackie's work, and would be honored to have her as a client.

"Should I sign with him?" Jackie asked me afterward.

"Of course," I said. "How else can you support me?" She signed. Rhys has already got her booked for a solo spring appearance at Carnegie, not the little recital hall but the big hall. Even after his cut, the fee for the one concert is twice what Jackie earned from teaching all last year.

The day after our concert checks arrived, we held a special meeting of the Antiqua Players. We were going to hold it at Monza's and let Terry's uncle cook us dinner, but at the last minute a big wedding party called up and reserved the entire main dining room, so we gathered at the studio instead. Everybody congratulated Jackie, but the same question was on everybody's mind, including mine. David was the one who actually asked it. "Now what?" he said to Jackie. "What happens now?"

"What do you mean?" Jackie asked him.

"Now that you're a big shot," David said, "are you going to be playing with us any more? Are *we* going to stay together?" Jackie's eyes began to flash dangerously.

"What kind of a person do you think I am?" she demanded. "Of course there's going to keep on being an Antiqua Players, and of course I'm going to keep on playing with you. Unless you kick me out. And don't you *dare* think anything different."

"Okay, okay," David muttered, "I was just asking."

179

"Well, you didn't have to ask," Jackie said tartly.

"You are all my children," I interrupted grandly, "and Miss Craine will have to interrupt her busy concert schedule to return to the bosom of the family. Now, let's eat."

The next day, Ralph, David, and Terry all took off for Antigua. They're no fools. The day after that, we got thirteen inches of snow in New York. Jackie came uptown, and we played a little music on the tape-deck and stir-fried some stringbeans and wound up the pig and let it dance for us.

"How would Hoboken be for a honeymoon?" I asked her.

"We can ask around," she said, "as soon as I get done with this big gig in the spring."

JAMES GOLLIN

James Gollin began piano lessons at age nine, became interested in preclassical music in college, and knows first hand not only music but the working life of the professional musician.

In addition to the three Antiqua Players suspense novels, THE PHILOMEL FOUNDATION, ELIZA'S GALIARDO, and THE VERONA PASSAMEZZO, he has written three acclaimed nonfiction works, PAY NOW, DIE LATER; WORLDLY GOODS; and THE STAR SPANGLED RETIREMENT DREAM.

Mr. Gollin, married and the father of two sons, lives in northern Westchester.

THE LIBRARY OF CRIME CLASSICS®

George Baxt
THE DOROTHY PARKER
MURDER CASE
0-930330-36-6   288pp $4.95

A QUEER KIND OF DEATH
0-930330-46-3   250pp $4.95

A PARADE OF COCKEYED
CREATURES
0-930330-47-1   250pp $4.95

Anthony Boucher
NINE TIMES NINE
0-930330-37-4   256pp $4.95

Caryl Brahms & S.J. Simon
A BULLET IN THE BALLET
0-930330-12-9   159pp $4.95

MURDER A LA STROGANOFF
0-930330-33-1   274pp $4.95

SIX CURTAINS FOR
STROGANOVA
0-930330-49-8   250pp $4.95

Christianna Brand
CAT AND MOUSE
0-930330-18-8   200pp $4.95

John Dickson Carr
BELOW SUSPICION
0-930330-50-1   186pp $4.95

THE BURNING COURT
0-930330-27-7   215pp $4.95

DEATH TURNS THE TABLES
0-930330-22-6   200pp $4.95

HAG'S NOOK
0-930330-28-5   192pp $4.95

HE WHO WHISPERS
0-930330-38-2   176pp $4.95

THE PROBLEM OF THE
GREEN CAPSULE
0-930330-51-X   223pp $4.95

THE SLEEPING SPHINX
0-930330-24-2   199pp $4.95

THE THREE COFFINS
0-930330-39-0   256pp $4.95

TILL DEATH DO US PART
0-930330-21-8   200pp $4.95

Carroll John Daly
MURDER FROM THE EAST
0-930330-01-3   312pp $4.95

Lillian De La Torre
DR. SAM: JOHNSON, DETECTOR
0-930330-08-0   261pp $4.95

THE DETECTIONS OF
DR. SAM: JOHNSON
0-930330-09-9   190pp $4.95

THE RETURN OF DR. SAM:
JOHNSON, DETECTOR
0-930330-34-X   200pp $4.95

**Dashiell Hammett
& Alex Raymond**
SECRET AGENT X-9
0-930330-05-6   225pp $9.95

James Gollin
ELIZA'S GALIARDO
0-930330-40-4   180pp $4.95

THE PHILOMEL FOUNDATION
0-930330-40-4   208pp $4.95

Richard Hull
THE MURDER OF MY AUNT
0-930330-02-1   174pp $4.95

Victoria Lincoln
A PRIVATE DISGRACE
LIZZIE BORDEN BY DAYLIGHT
0-930330-35-8   320pp $5.95

Barry N. Malzberg
UNDERLAY
0-930330-41-2   256pp $4.95

Margaret Millar
AN AIR THAT KILLS
0-930330-23-4   247pp $4.95

ASK FOR ME TOMORROW
0-930330-15-3   179pp $4.95

BANSHEE
0-930330-14-5   202pp $4.95

BEAST IN VIEW
0-930330-07-2   251pp $4.95

BEYOND THIS POINT
ARE MONSTERS
0-930330-31-5   213pp $4.95

THE CANNIBAL HEART
0-930330-32-3   207pp $4.95

THE FIEND
0-930330-10-2   245pp $4.95

HOW LIKE AN ANGEL
0-930330-04-8   279pp $4.95

THE LISTENING WALLS
0-930330-52-8   250pp $4.95

A STRANGER IN MY GRAVE
0-930330-06-4   311pp $4.95

ROSE'S LAST SUMMER
0-930330-26-9   223pp $4.95

WALL OF EYES
0-930330-42-0   224pp $4.95

William F. Nolan
SPACE FOR HIRE
0-930330-19-6   200pp $4.95

LOOK OUT FOR SPACE
0-930330-20-X   192pp $4.95

Ellery Queen
THE TRAGEDY OF X
0-930330-43-9   256pp $4.95

THE TRAGEDY OF Y
0-930330-53-6   244pp $4.95

Clayton Rawson
DEATH FROM A TOP HAT
0-930330-44-7   288pp $4.95

S.S. Rafferty
CORK OF THE COLONIES
0-930330-11-0   314pp $4.95

DIE LAUGHING
0-930330-16-1   200pp $4.95

John Sherwood
A SHOT IN THE ARM
0-930330-25-0   172pp $4.95

Hake Talbot
RIM OF THE PIT
0-930330-30-7   278pp $4.95

Darwin L. Teilhet
THE TALKING SPARROW
MURDERS
0-930330-29-3   301pp $4.95